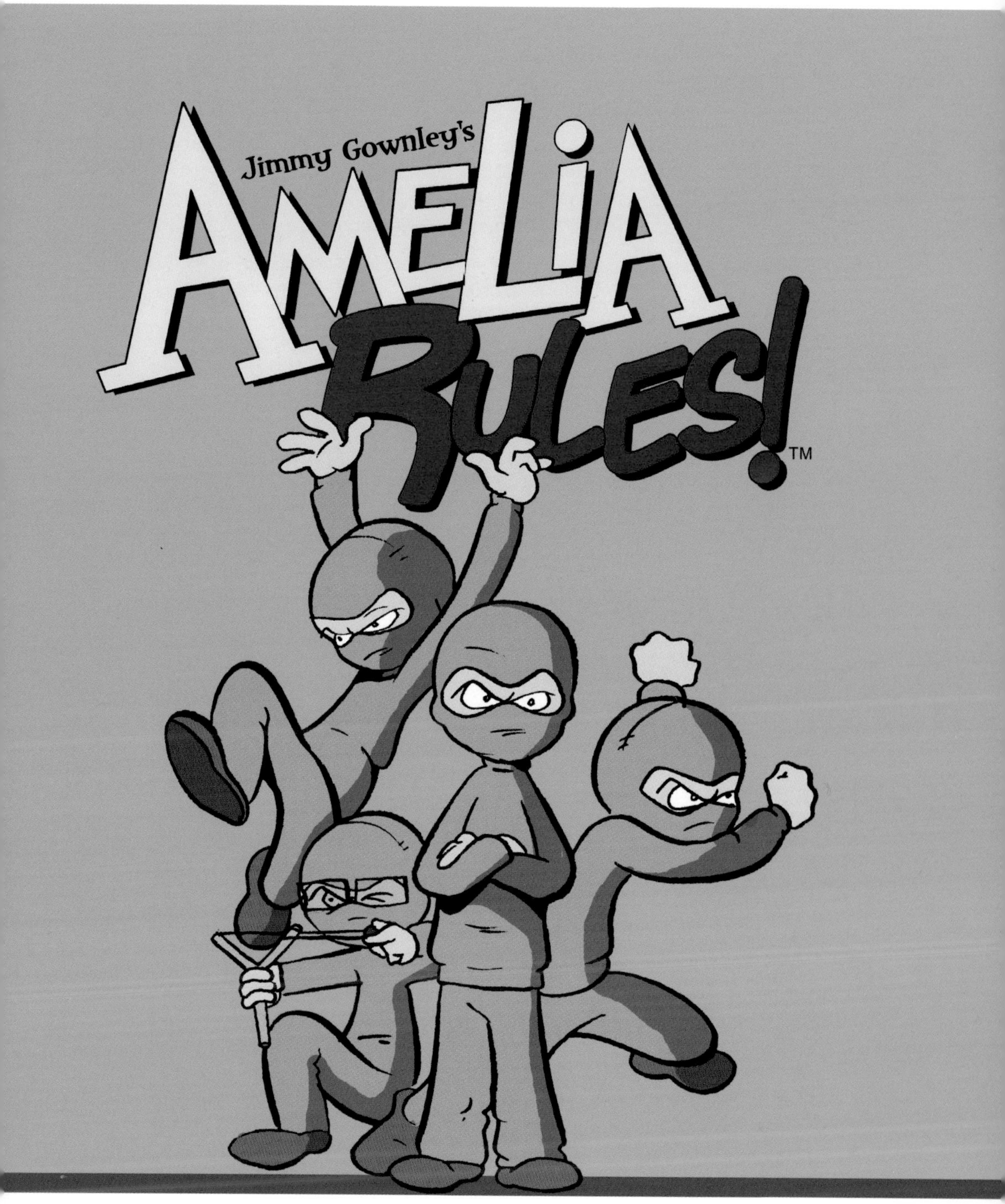
Jimmy Gownley's
AMELIA RULES!
TM

Fireflies and Time

Atheneum Books for Young Readers
New York London Toronto Sydney

Spotlight

visit us at www.abdopublishing.com

Reinforced library bound edition published in 2013 by Spotlight, a division of the ABDO Group, PO Box 398166, Minneapolis, MN 55439. Spotlight produces high-quality reinforced library bound editions for schools and libraries. Published by agreement with Atheneum Books for Young Readers, an imprint of Simon & Schuster Children's Publishing Division.

Printed in the United States of America, North Mankato, Minnesota.
102012
012013
This book contains at least 10% recycled materials.

This book is a work of fiction. Any references to historical events, real people, or real locales are used fictitiously. Other names, characters, places, and incidents are products of the author's imagination, and any resemblance to actual events or locales or persons, living or dead, is entirely coincidental.

Book design by Sonia Chaghatzbanian

Library of Congress Cataloging-in-Publication Data

Gownley, Jimmy.
Amelia in fireflies and time / [Jimmy Gownley]. -- Reinforced library bound ed.
p. cm. -- (Jimmy Gownley's Amelia rules!)
Summary: As fourth grade comes to an end, Reggie, Rhonda, and Amelia let their imaginations soar.
ISBN 978-1-61479-069-3
[1. Graphic novels. 2. Imagination--Fiction. 3. Friendship--Fiction.] I. Title.
PZ7.7.G69Ami 2013
741.5'973--dc23

2012026903

To Major Stephen M. Murphy.
This book is for you, with thanks
for your service to our country,
and for your friendship.

MEET THE GANG

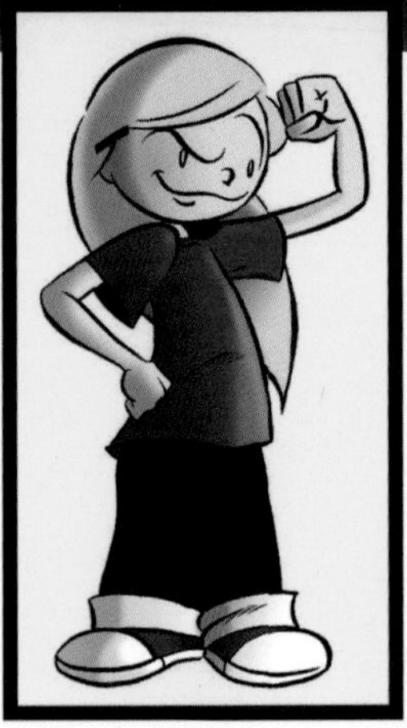

Amelia Louise McBride:
Our heroine. Wise cracking, yet sweet. She spends her time hanging out with friends and her aunt Tanner.

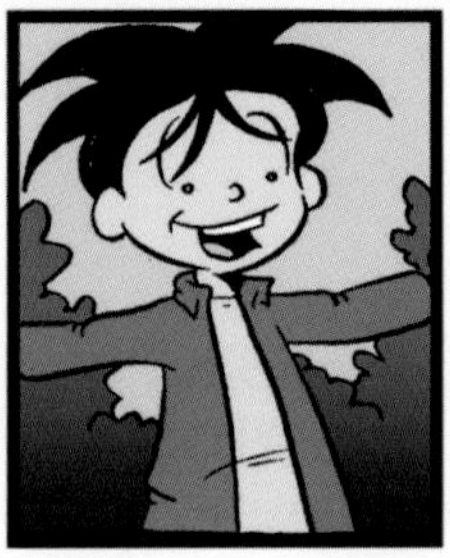

Reggie Grabinsky:
A.k.a. Captain Amazing. Founder of G.A.S.P., which he forces . . . er, encourages, his friends to join.

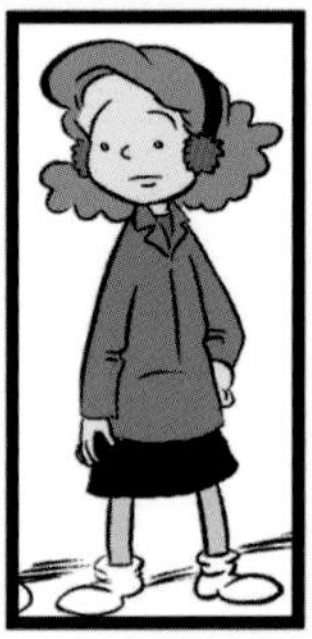

Rhonda Bleenie:
Smart, stubborn, and loud. She wears her heart on her sleeve and it's filled with love for Reggie.

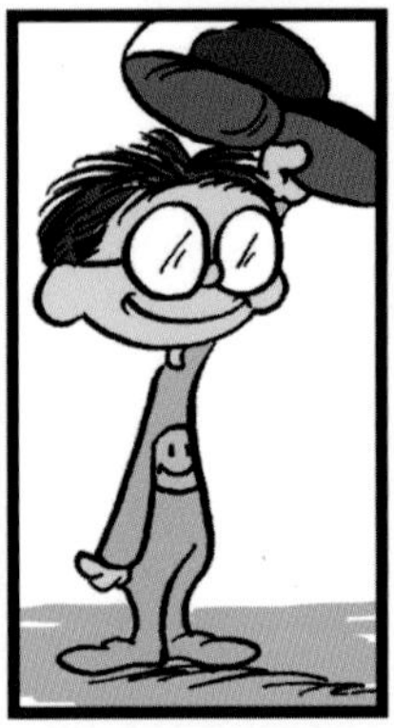

Pajamaman:
Never speaks. Always cool. His feetie jammies tell you what's on his mind.

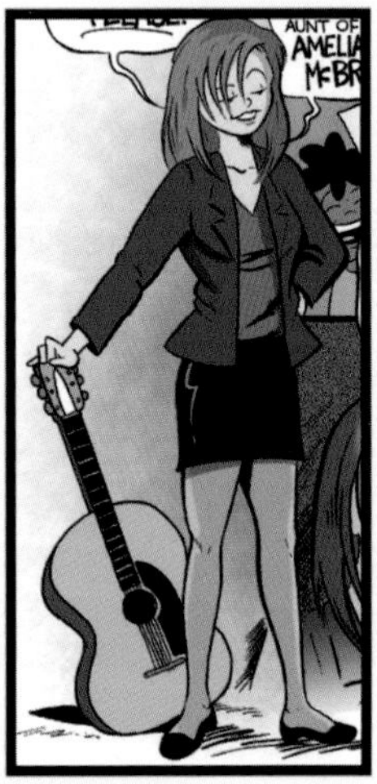
AUNT OF
AMELIA

Tanner:
Amelia's aunt and a former rock 'n' roll superstar.

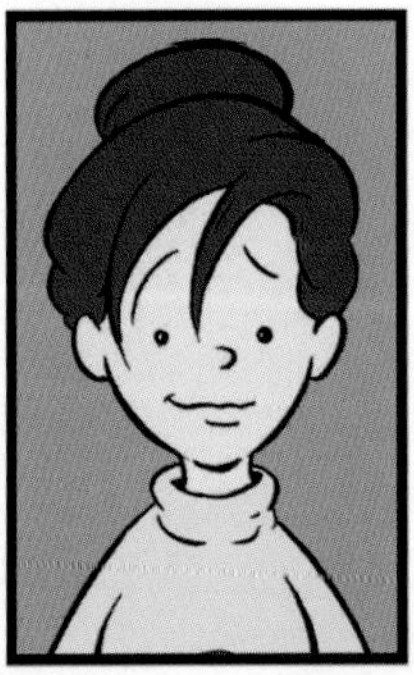

Amelia's Mom (Mary):
Starting a new life in Pennsylvania with Amelia after the divorce.

Amelia's Dad:
Still lives in New York, and misses Amelia terribly.

G.A.S.P.
Gathering Of Awesome Super Pals. The superhero club Reggie founded.

Park View Terrace Ninjas:
Club across town and nemesis to G.A.S.P.

Kyle:
The main ninja. Kind of a jerk but not without charm.

Joan:
Former Park View Terrace Ninja (nemesis of G.A.S.P.), now friends with Amelia and company.

Tweenie Zeenie:
A local kid-run magazine and Web site.

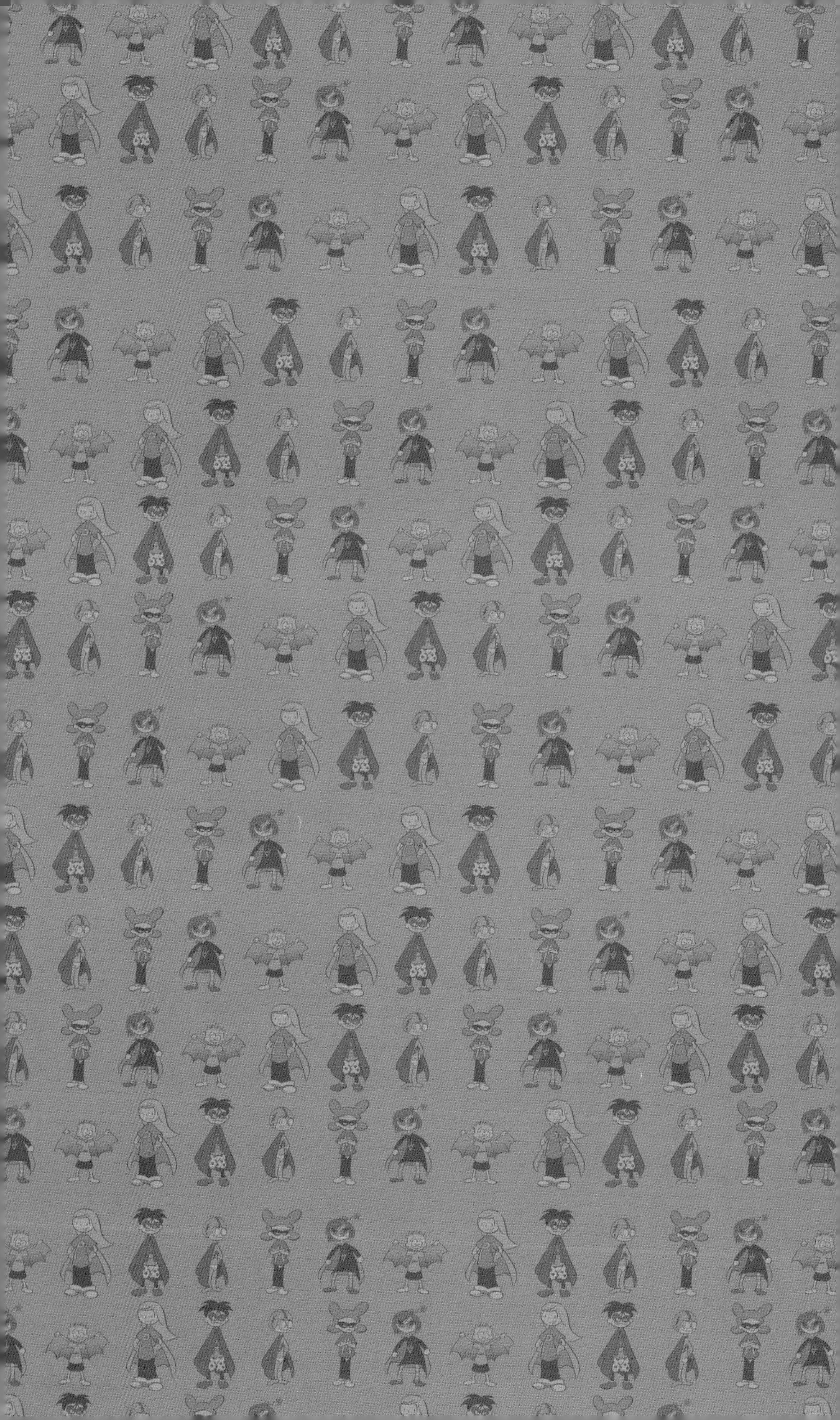

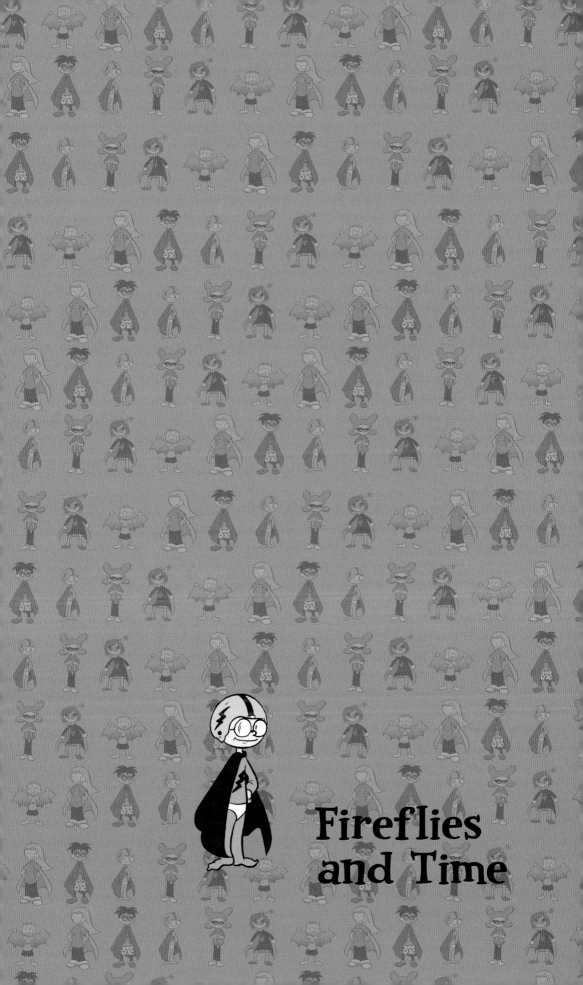

Fireflies
and Time

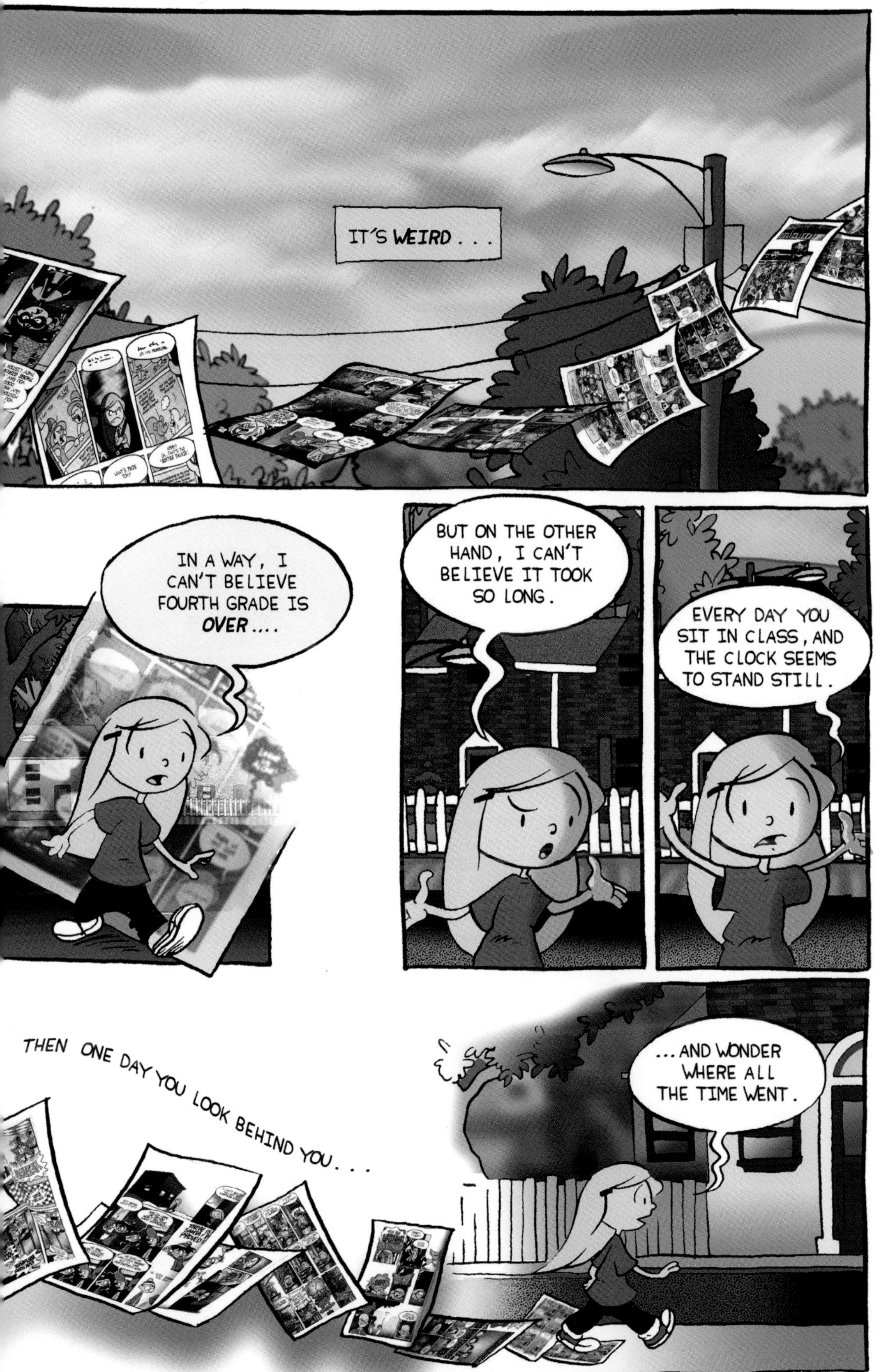
IT'S **WEIRD** . . .
IN A WAY, I CAN'T BELIEVE FOURTH GRADE IS ***OVER***....
BUT ON THE OTHER HAND, I CAN'T BELIEVE IT TOOK SO LONG.
EVERY DAY YOU SIT IN CLASS, AND THE CLOCK SEEMS TO STAND STILL.
THEN ONE DAY YOU LOOK BEHIND YOU . . .
...AND WONDER WHERE ALL THE TIME WENT.

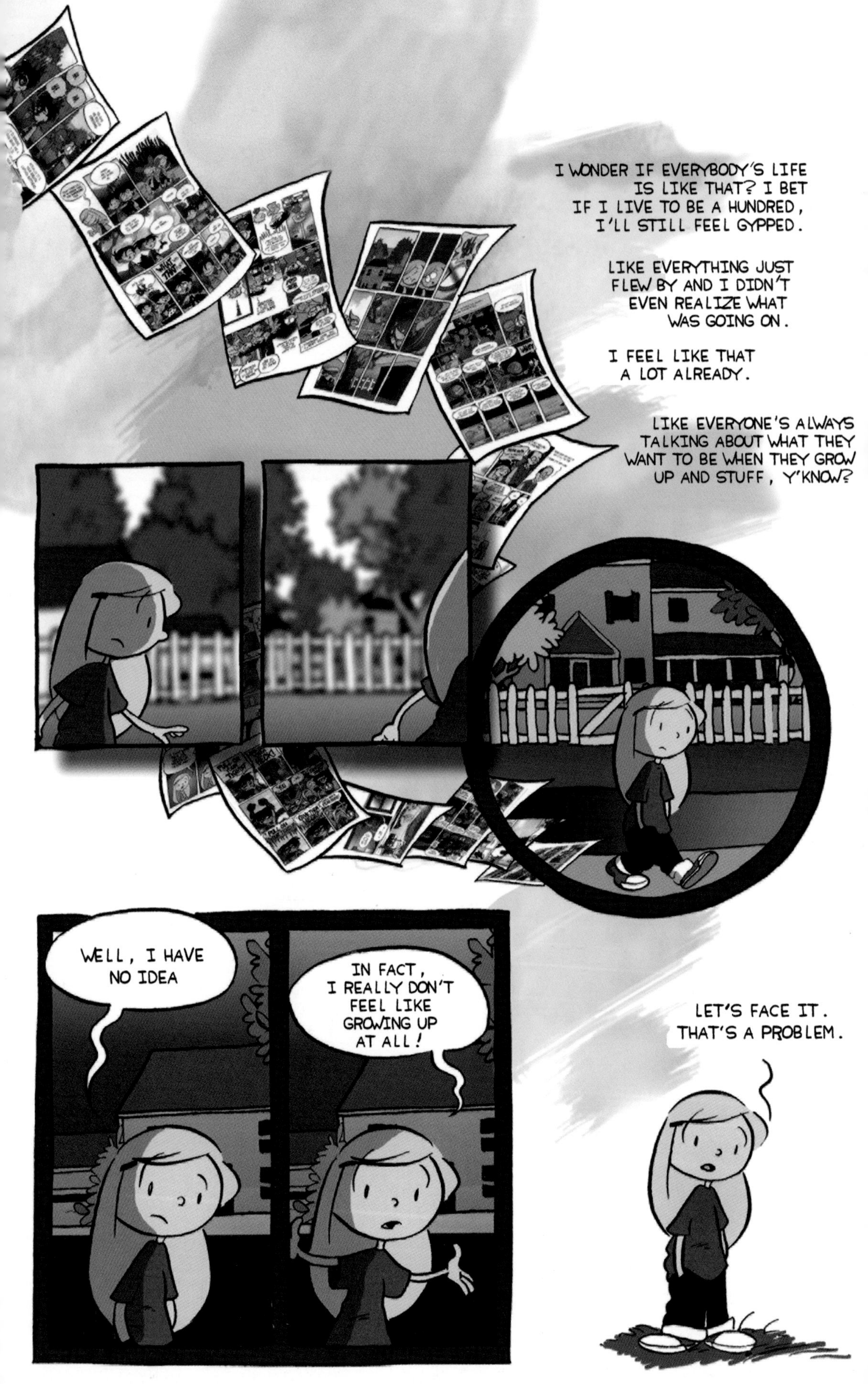
I WONDER IF EVERYBODY'S LIFE IS LIKE THAT? I BET IF I LIVE TO BE A HUNDRED, I'LL STILL FEEL GYPPED.
LIKE EVERYTHING JUST FLEW BY AND I DIDN'T EVEN REALIZE WHAT WAS GOING ON.
I FEEL LIKE THAT A LOT ALREADY.
LIKE EVERYONE'S ALWAYS TALKING ABOUT WHAT THEY WANT TO BE WHEN THEY GROW UP AND STUFF, Y'KNOW?
WELL, I HAVE NO IDEA
IN FACT, I REALLY DON'T FEEL LIKE GROWING UP AT ALL!
LET'S FACE IT. THAT'S A PROBLEM.

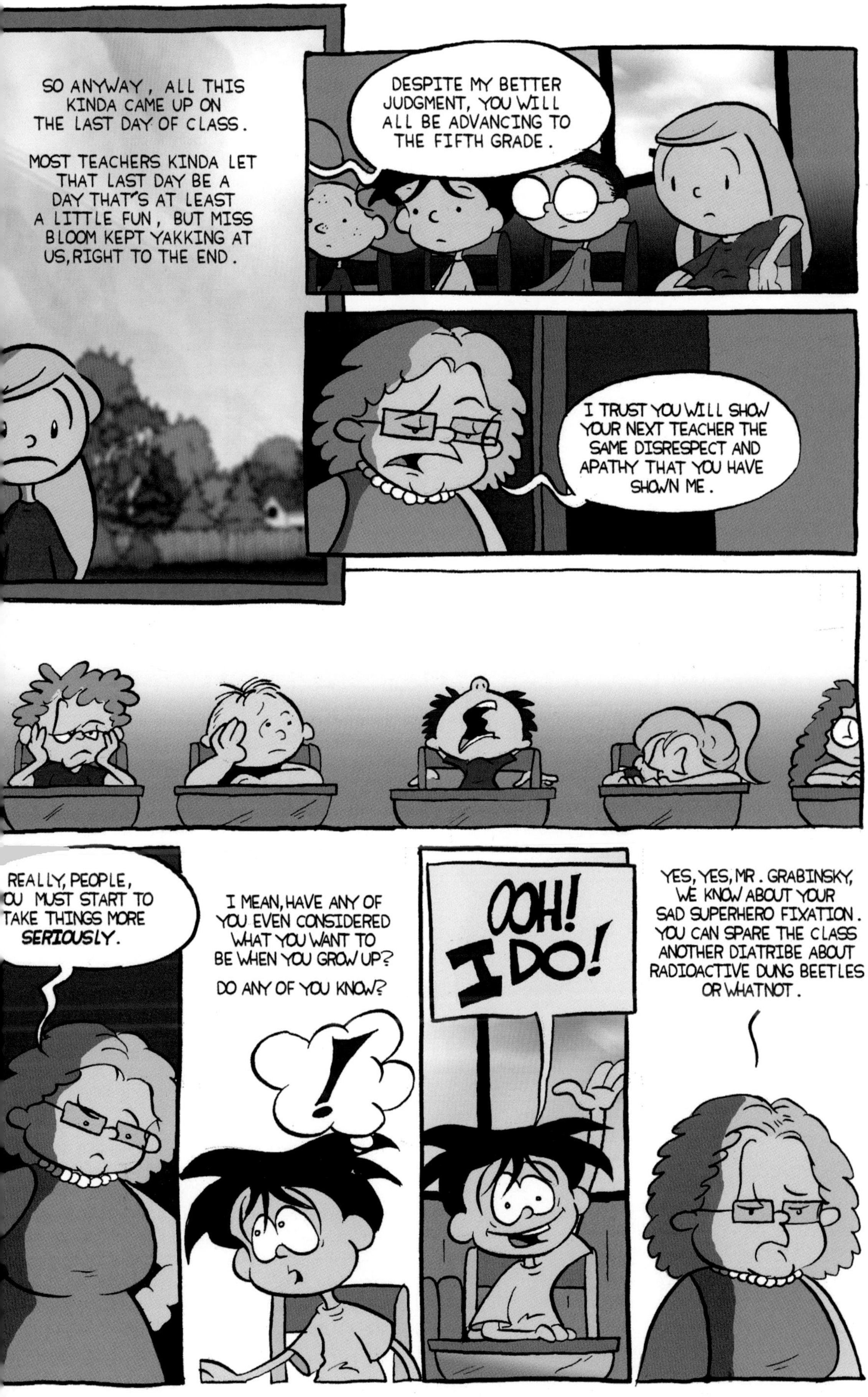
SO ANYWAY, ALL THIS KINDA CAME UP ON THE LAST DAY OF CLASS.
MOST TEACHERS KINDA LET THAT LAST DAY BE A DAY THAT'S AT LEAST A LITTLE FUN, BUT MISS BLOOM KEPT YAKKING AT US, RIGHT TO THE END.
DESPITE MY BETTER JUDGMENT, YOU WILL ALL BE ADVANCING TO THE FIFTH GRADE.
I TRUST YOU WILL SHOW YOUR NEXT TEACHER THE SAME DISRESPECT AND APATHY THAT YOU HAVE SHOWN ME.
REALLY, PEOPLE, OU MUST START TO TAKE THINGS MORE SERIOUSLY.
I MEAN, HAVE ANY OF YOU EVEN CONSIDERED WHAT YOU WANT TO BE WHEN YOU GROW UP?
DO ANY OF YOU KNOW?
!
OOH! I DO!
YES, YES, MR. GRABINSKY, WE KNOW ABOUT YOUR SAD SUPERHERO FIXATION. YOU CAN SPARE THE CLASS ANOTHER DIATRIBE ABOUT RADIOACTIVE DUNG BEETLES OR WHATNOT.

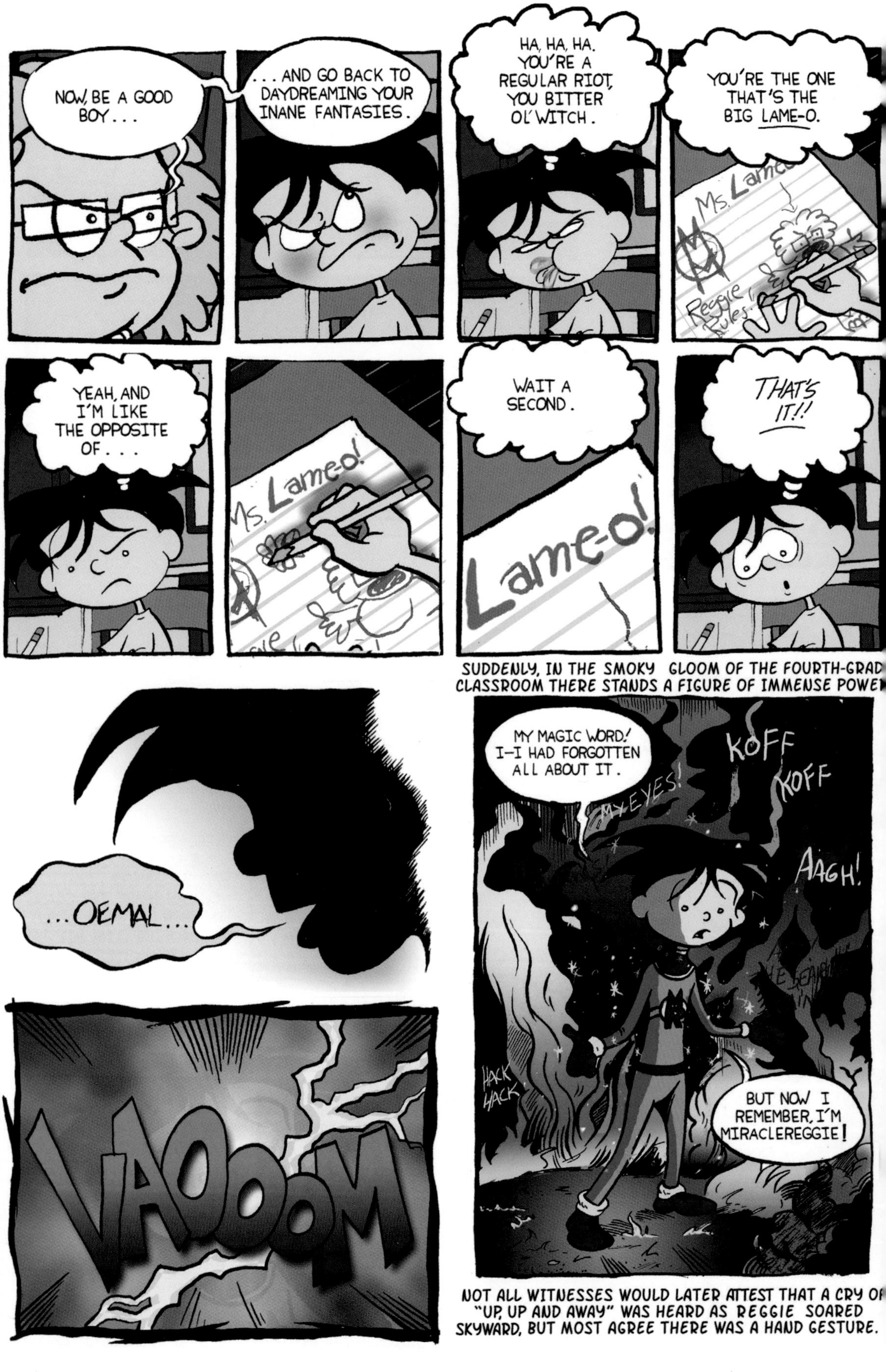
NOW, BE A GOOD BOY . . .
. . . AND GO BACK TO DAYDREAMING YOUR INANE FANTASIES .
HA, HA, HA. YOU'RE A REGULAR RIOT, YOU BITTER OL' WITCH .
YOU'RE THE ONE THAT'S THE BIG LAME-O.
Ms. Lame-o
Reggie Rules!
YEAH, AND I'M LIKE THE OPPOSITE OF . . .
Ms. Lame-o!
WAIT A SECOND .
Lame-o!
THAT'S IT!!
. . . OEMAL . . .
VAOOOOM
SUDDENLY, IN THE SMOKY GLOOM OF THE FOURTH-GRAD
CLASSROOM THERE STANDS A FIGURE OF IMMENSE POWE
MY MAGIC WORD! I—I HAD FORGOTTEN ALL ABOUT IT .
MY EYES!
KOFF
KOFF
AAGH!
HACK
HACK
BUT NOW I REMEMBER, I'M MIRACLEREGGIE!
NOT ALL WITNESSES WOULD LATER ATTEST THAT A CRY OF
"UP, UP AND AWAY" WAS HEARD AS REGGIE SOARED
SKYWARD, BUT MOST AGREE THERE WAS A HAND GESTURE.

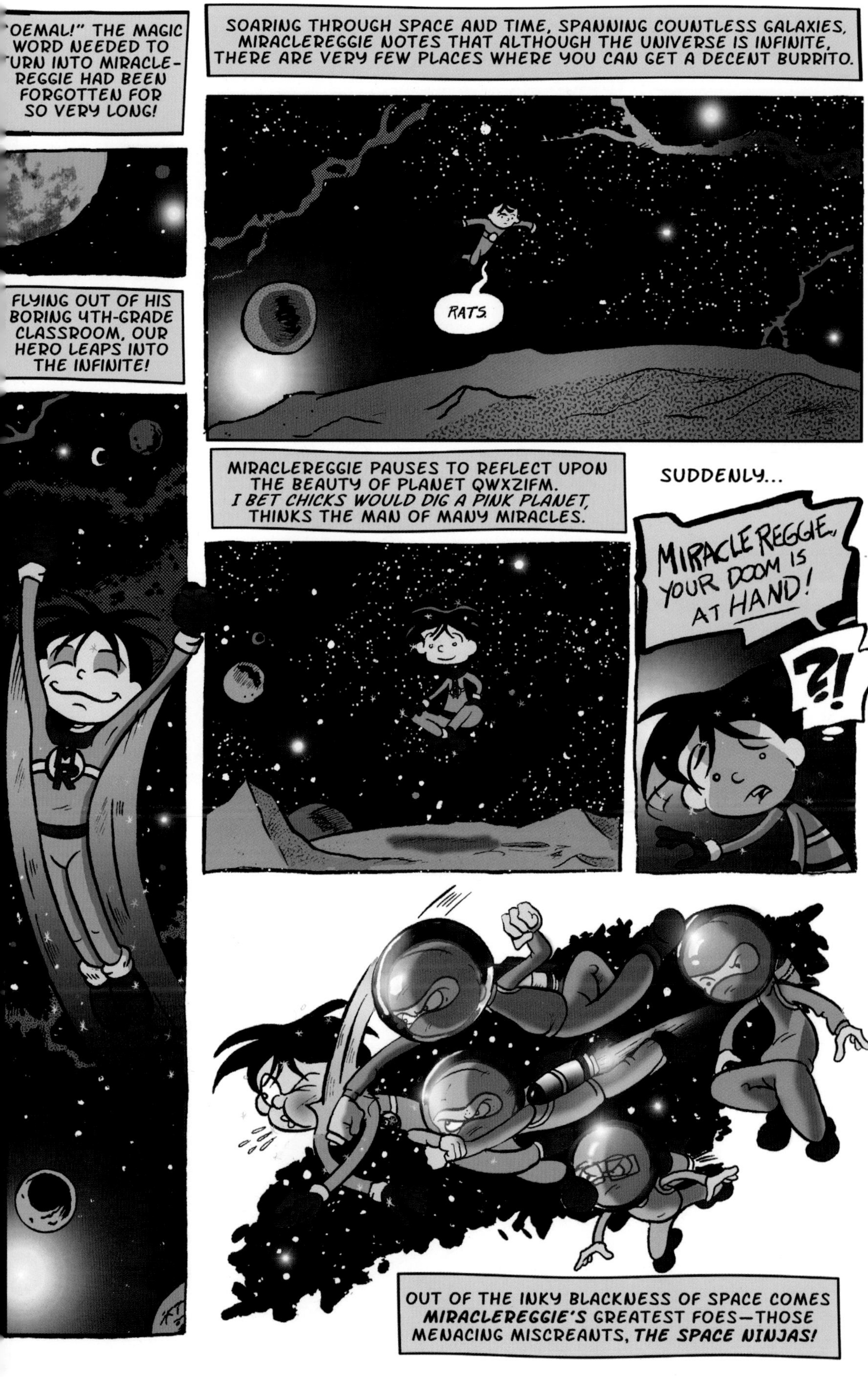
"OEMAL!" THE MAGIC WORD NEEDED TO URN INTO MIRACLE-REGGIE HAD BEEN FORGOTTEN FOR SO VERY LONG!
FLYING OUT OF HIS BORING 4TH-GRADE CLASSROOM, OUR HERO LEAPS INTO THE INFINITE!
SOARING THROUGH SPACE AND TIME, SPANNING COUNTLESS GALAXIES, MIRACLEREGGIE NOTES THAT ALTHOUGH THE UNIVERSE IS INFINITE, THERE ARE VERY FEW PLACES WHERE YOU CAN GET A DECENT BURRITO.
RATS.
MIRACLEREGGIE PAUSES TO REFLECT UPON THE BEAUTY OF PLANET QWXZIFM. *I BET CHICKS WOULD DIG A PINK PLANET,* THINKS THE MAN OF MANY MIRACLES.
SUDDENLY...
MIRACLEREGGIE, YOUR DOOM IS AT HAND!
?!
OUT OF THE INKY BLACKNESS OF SPACE COMES ***MIRACLEREGGIE'S*** GREATEST FOES—THOSE MENACING MISCREANTS, ***THE SPACE NINJAS!***

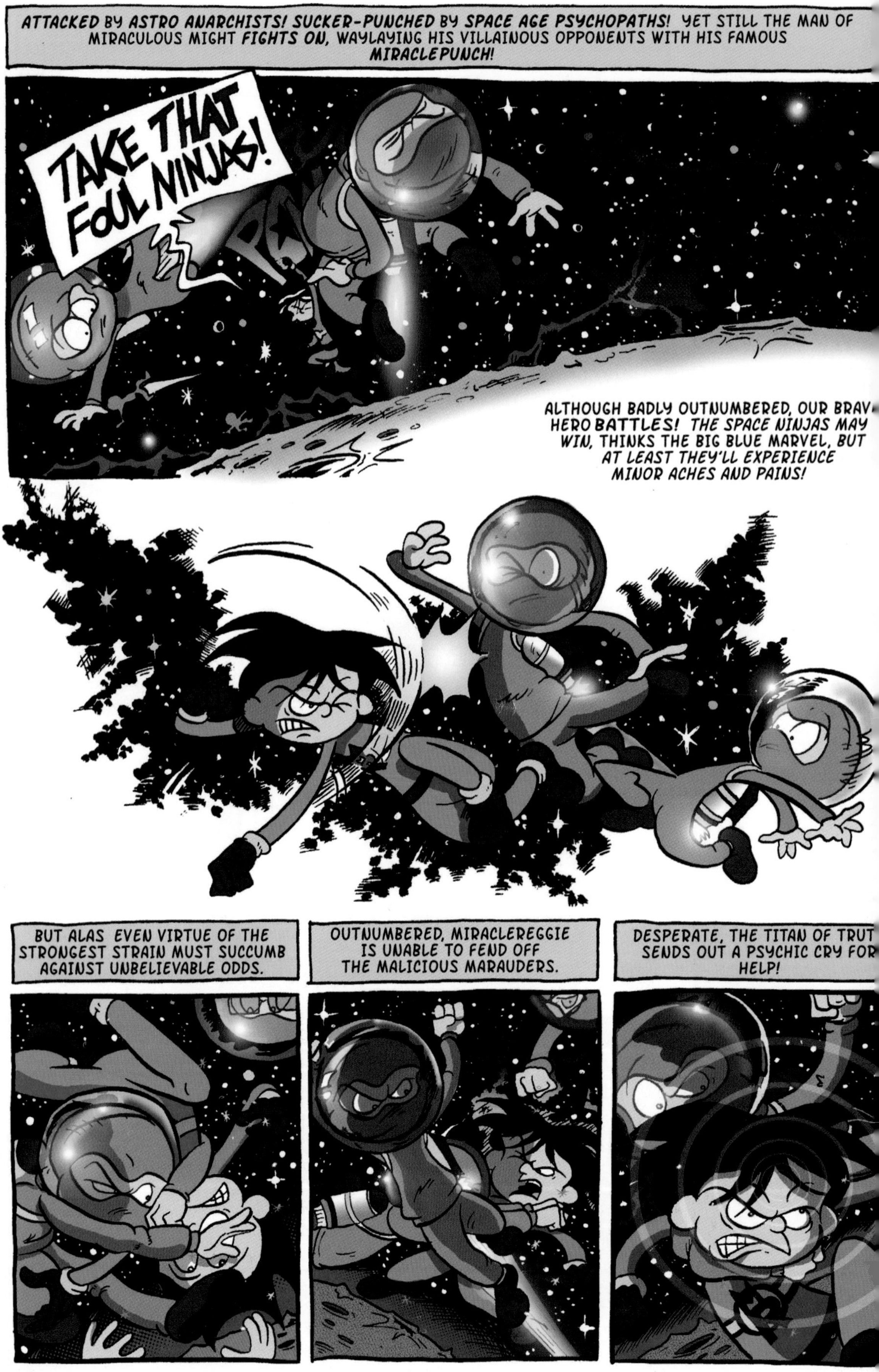
ATTACKED BY ASTRO ANARCHISTS! SUCKER-PUNCHED BY SPACE AGE PSYCHOPATHS! YET STILL THE MAN OF MIRACULOUS MIGHT FIGHTS ON, WAYLAYING HIS VILLAINOUS OPPONENTS WITH HIS FAMOUS MIRACLEPUNCH!
TAKE THAT FOUL NINJAS!
ALTHOUGH BADLY OUTNUMBERED, OUR BRAV HERO BATTLES! THE SPACE NINJAS MAY WIN, THINKS THE BIG BLUE MARVEL, BUT AT LEAST THEY'LL EXPERIENCE MINOR ACHES AND PAINS!
BUT ALAS EVEN VIRTUE OF THE STRONGEST STRAIN MUST SUCCUMB AGAINST UNBELIEVABLE ODDS.
OUTNUMBERED, MIRACLEREGGIE IS UNABLE TO FEND OFF THE MALICIOUS MARAUDERS.
DESPERATE, THE TITAN OF TRUT SENDS OUT A PSYCHIC CRY FOR HELP!

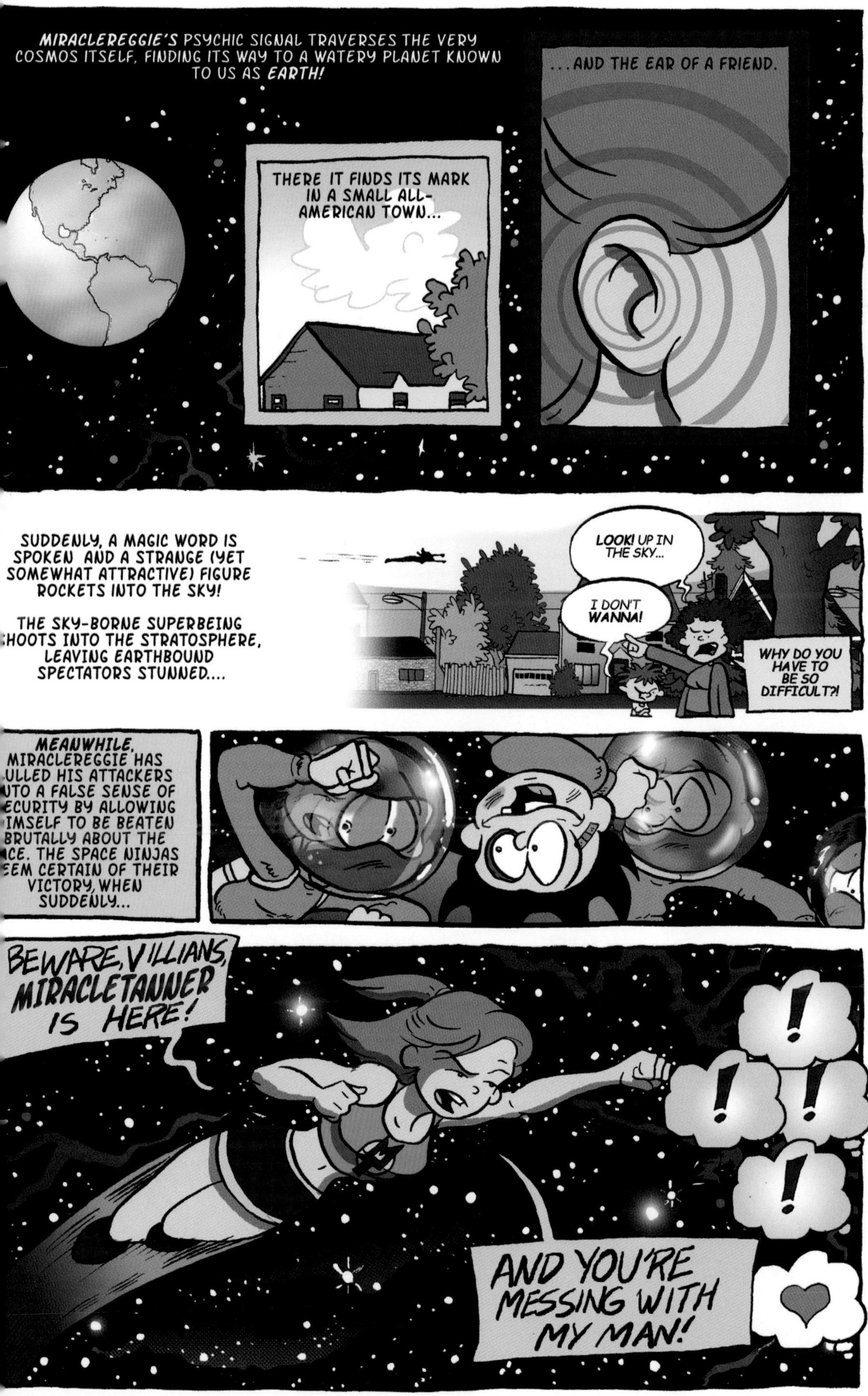
MIRACLEREGGIE'S PSYCHIC SIGNAL TRAVERSES THE VERY COSMOS ITSELF, FINDING ITS WAY TO A WATERY PLANET KNOWN TO US AS EARTH!
THERE IT FINDS ITS MARK IN A SMALL ALL-AMERICAN TOWN...
...AND THE EAR OF A FRIEND.
SUDDENLY, A MAGIC WORD IS SPOKEN AND A STRANGE (YET SOMEWHAT ATTRACTIVE) FIGURE ROCKETS INTO THE SKY!
THE SKY-BORNE SUPERBEING SHOOTS INTO THE STRATOSPHERE, LEAVING EARTHBOUND SPECTATORS STUNNED....
LOOK! UP IN THE SKY...
I DON'T WANNA!
WHY DO YOU HAVE TO BE SO DIFFICULT?!
MEANWHILE, MIRACLEREGGIE HAS LULLED HIS ATTACKERS INTO A FALSE SENSE OF SECURITY BY ALLOWING HIMSELF TO BE BEATEN BRUTALLY ABOUT THE FACE. THE SPACE NINJAS SEEM CERTAIN OF THEIR VICTORY, WHEN SUDDENLY...
BEWARE, VILLIANS, MIRACLETANNER IS HERE!
!
!
!
!
AND YOU'RE MESSING WITH MY MAN!

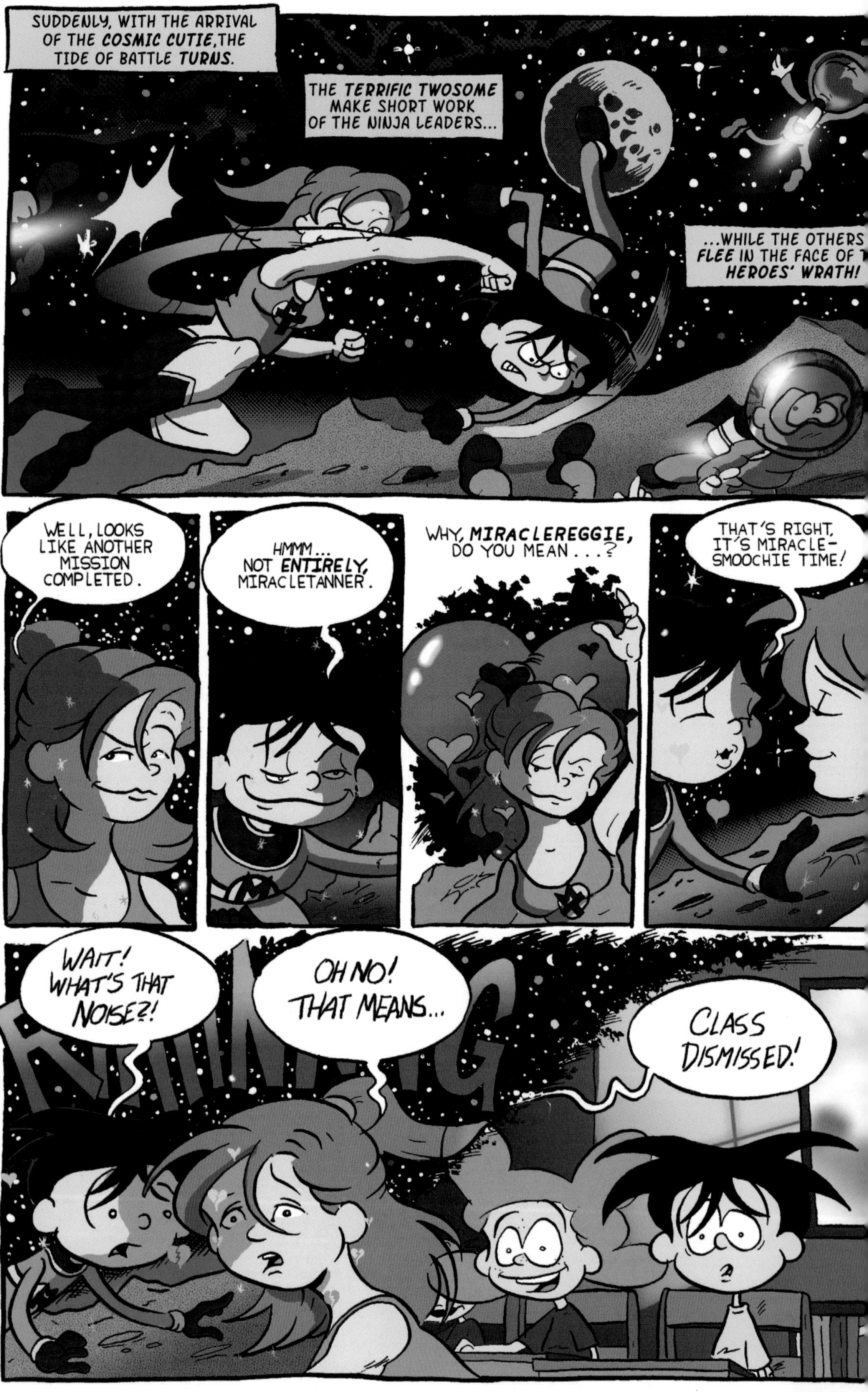

SUDDENLY, WITH THE ARRIVAL OF THE COSMIC CUTIE, THE TIDE OF BATTLE TURNS.
THE TERRIFIC TWOSOME MAKE SHORT WORK OF THE NINJA LEADERS...
...WHILE THE OTHERS FLEE IN THE FACE OF T HEROES' WRATH!
WELL, LOOKS LIKE ANOTHER MISSION COMPLETED.
HMMM... NOT ENTIRELY, MIRACLETANNER.
WHY, MIRACLEREGGIE, DO YOU MEAN...?
THAT'S RIGHT, IT'S MIRACLE-SMOOCHIE TIME!
WAIT! WHAT'S THAT NOISE?!
OH NO! THAT MEANS...
CLASS DISMISSED!

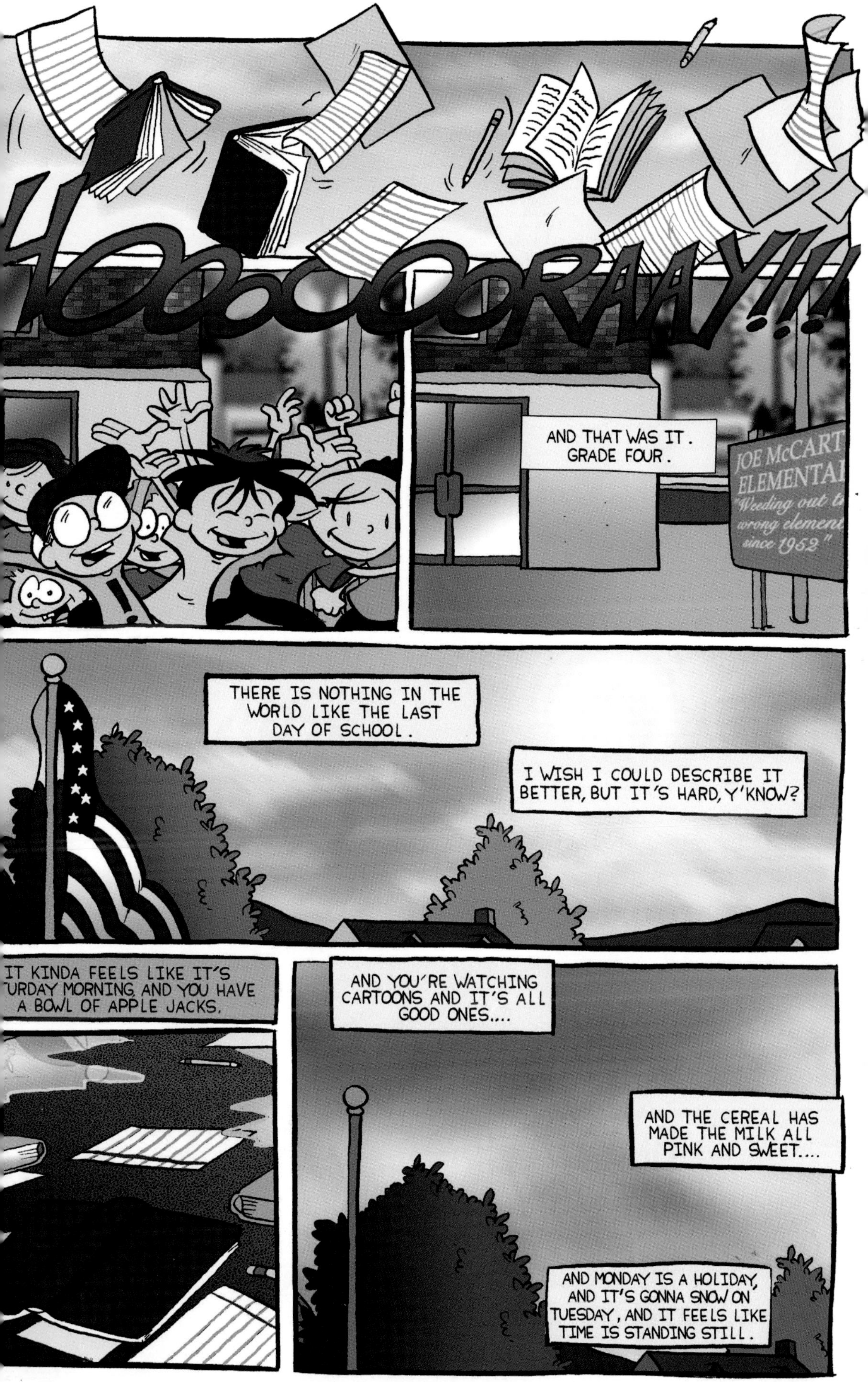
HOOOOOOORAAAY!!!
AND THAT WAS IT. GRADE FOUR.
JOE McCART
ELEMENTA
"Weeding out th
wrong element
since 1952"
THERE IS NOTHING IN THE WORLD LIKE THE LAST DAY OF SCHOOL.
I WISH I COULD DESCRIBE IT BETTER, BUT IT'S HARD, Y'KNOW?
IT KINDA FEELS LIKE IT'S
TURDAY MORNING, AND YOU HAVE A BOWL OF APPLE JACKS.
AND YOU'RE WATCHING CARTOONS AND IT'S ALL GOOD ONES....
AND THE CEREAL HAS MADE THE MILK ALL PINK AND SWEET....
AND MONDAY IS A HOLIDAY, AND IT'S GONNA SNOW ON TUESDAY, AND IT FEELS LIKE TIME IS STANDING STILL.

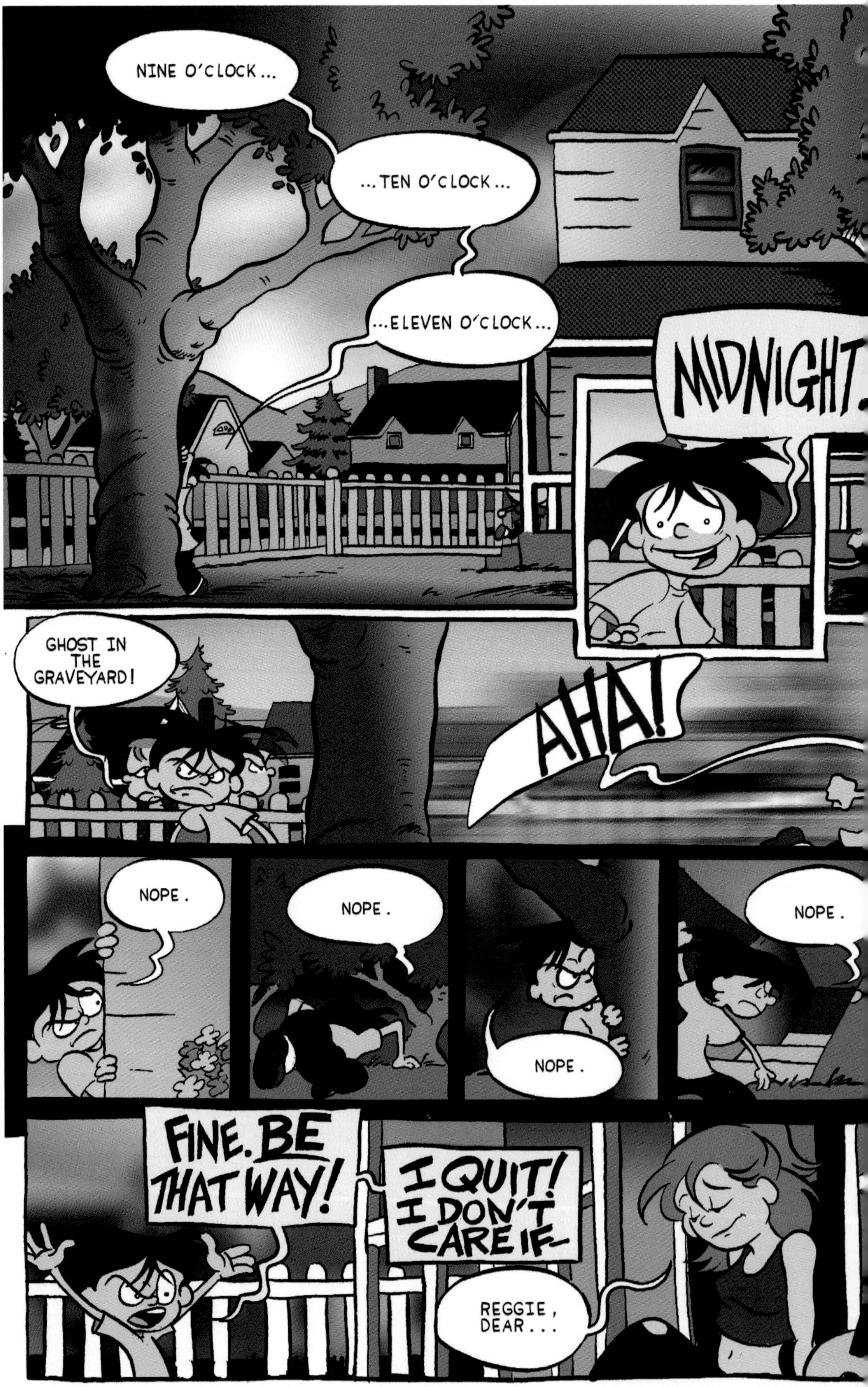
NINE O'CLOCK...
...TEN O'CLOCK...
...ELEVEN O'CLOCK...
MIDNIGHT.
GHOST IN THE GRAVEYARD!
AHA!
NOPE.
NOPE.
NOPE.
NOPE.
FINE. BE THAT WAY!
I QUIT! I DON'T CARE IF—
REGGIE, DEAR...

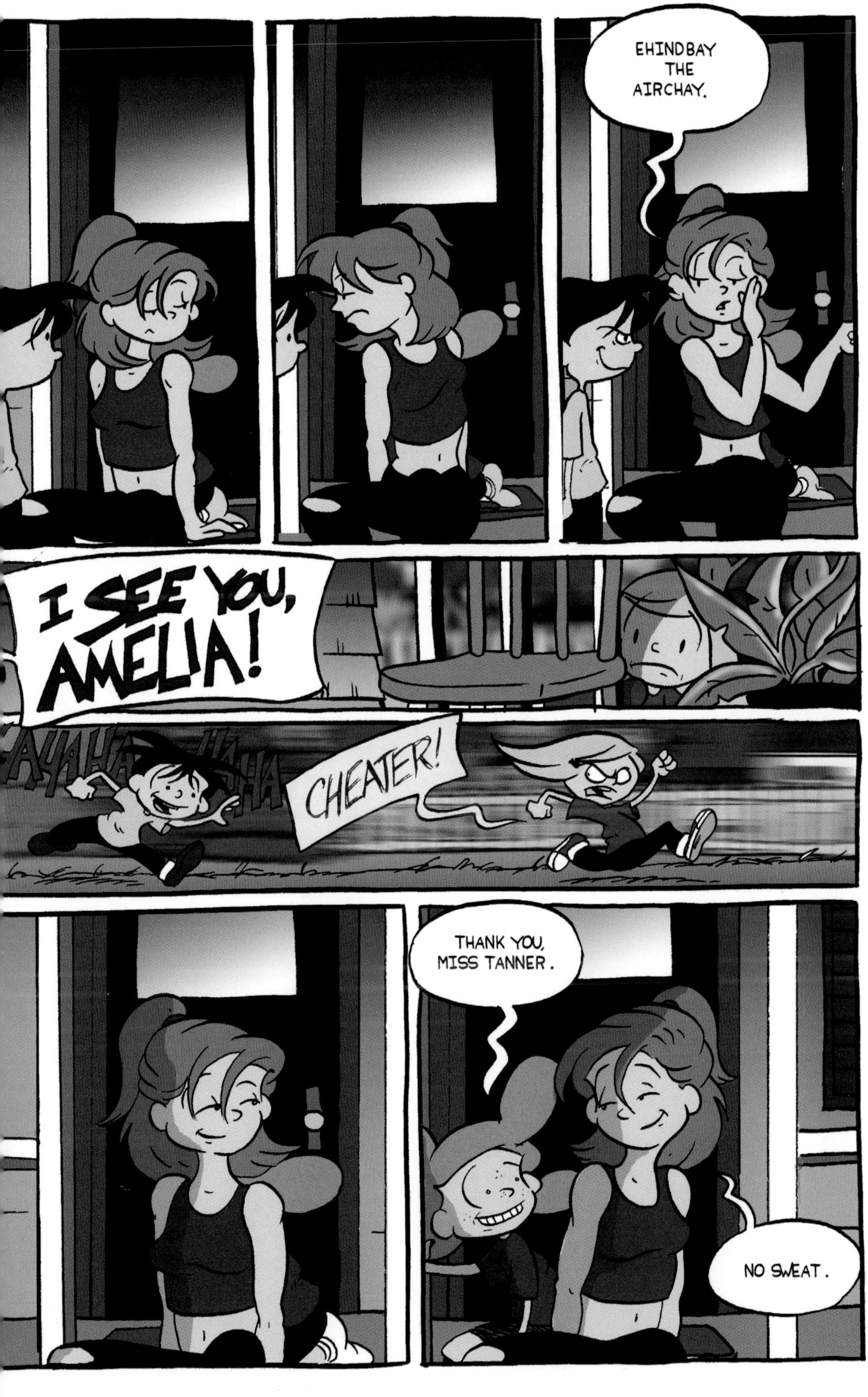
EHINDBAY THE AIRCHAY.
I SEE YOU, AMELIA!
AHAHA HAHA
CHEATER!
THANK YOU, MISS TANNER.
NO SWEAT.

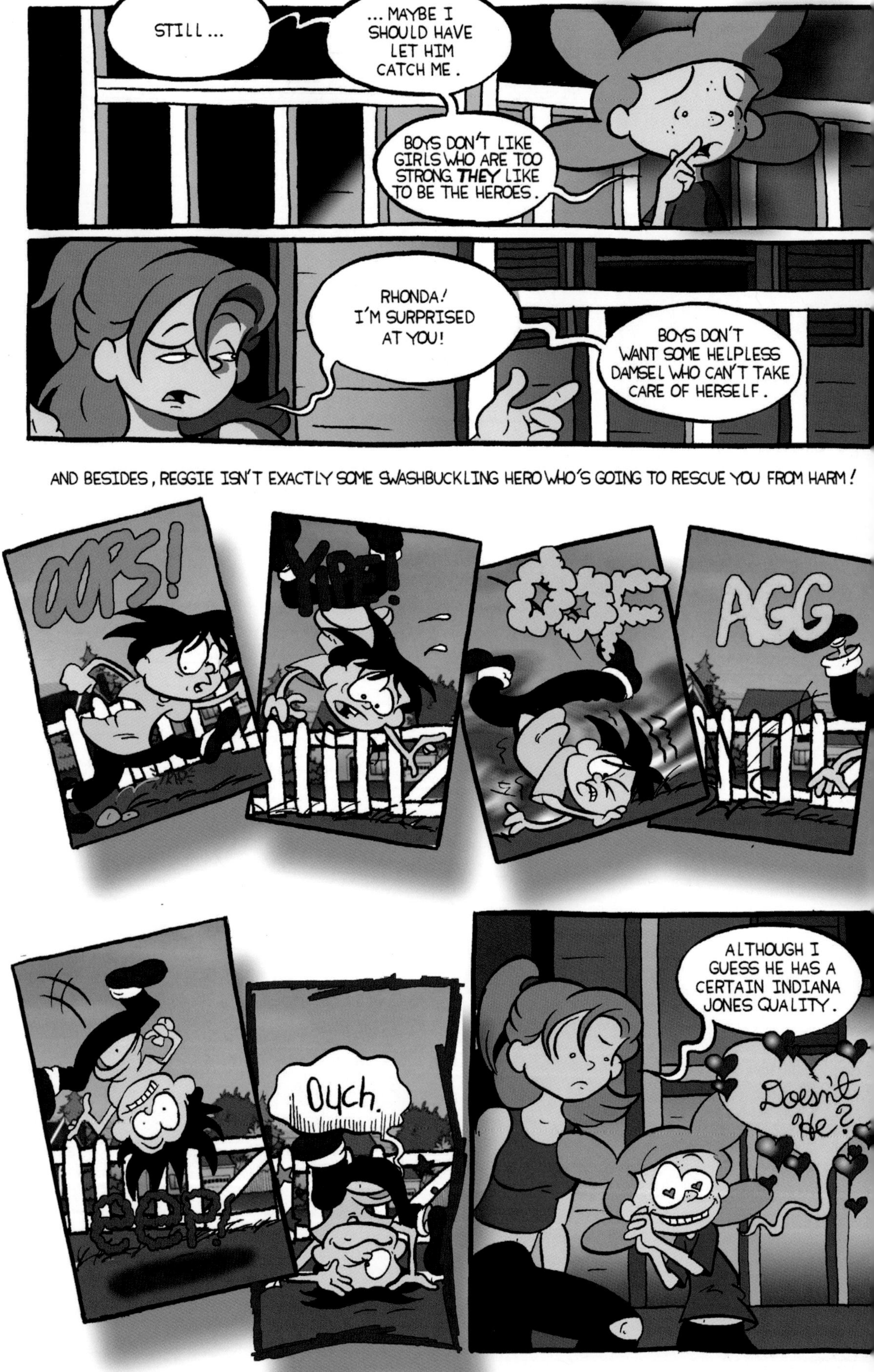
STILL...
...MAYBE I SHOULD HAVE LET HIM CATCH ME.
BOYS DON'T LIKE GIRLS WHO ARE TOO STRONG. **THEY** LIKE TO BE THE HEROES.
RHONDA! I'M SURPRISED AT YOU!
BOYS DON'T WANT SOME HELPLESS DAMSEL WHO CAN'T TAKE CARE OF HERSELF.
AND BESIDES, REGGIE ISN'T EXACTLY SOME SWASHBUCKLING HERO WHO'S GOING TO RESCUE YOU FROM HARM!
OOPS!
OOF
AGG
eep!
Ouch.
ALTHOUGH I GUESS HE HAS A CERTAIN INDIANA JONES QUALITY.
Doesn't He?

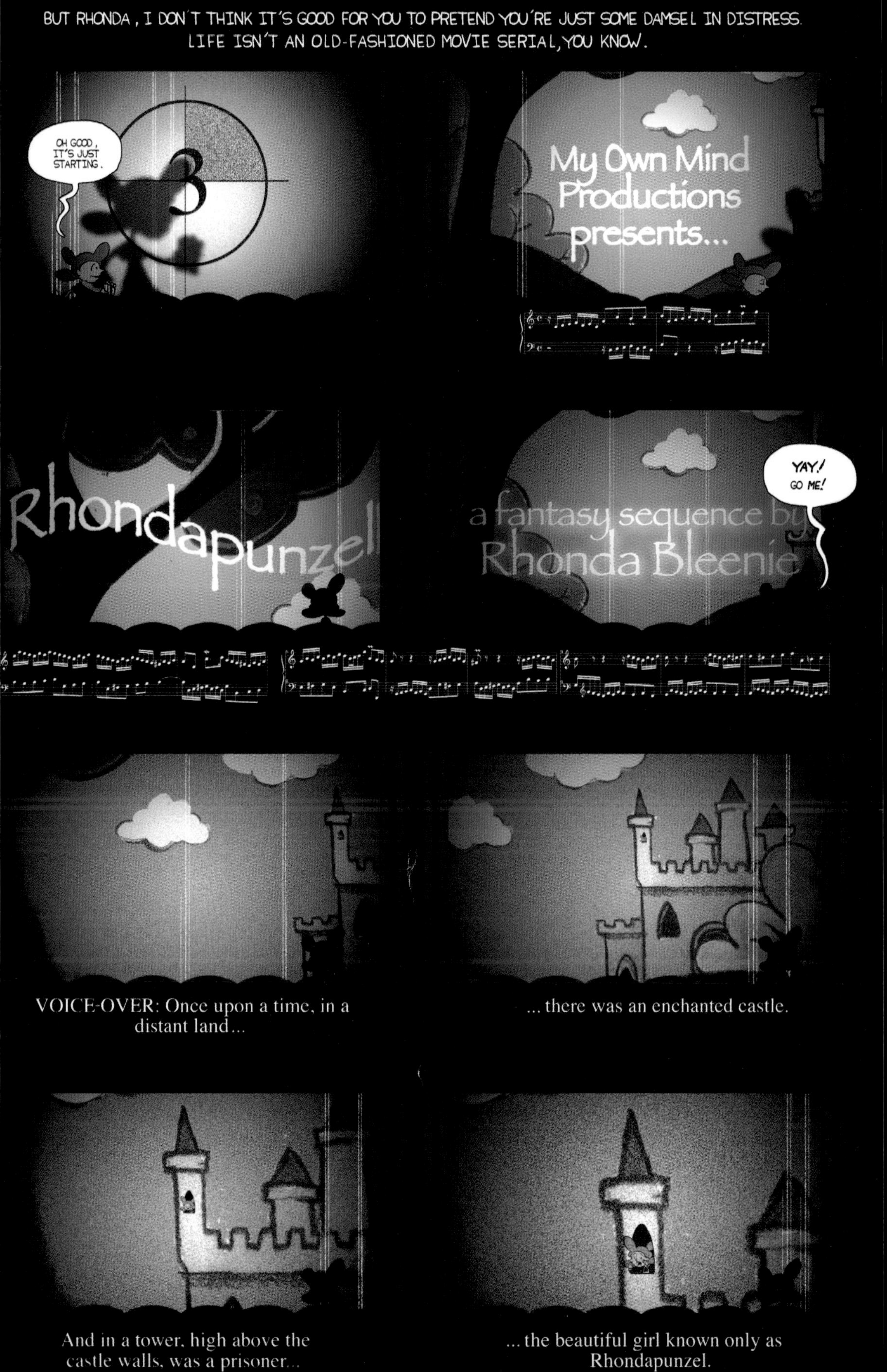

BUT RHONDA, I DON'T THINK IT'S GOOD FOR YOU TO PRETEND YOU'RE JUST SOME DAMSEL IN DISTRESS. LIFE ISN'T AN OLD-FASHIONED MOVIE SERIAL, YOU KNOW.
OH GOOD, IT'S JUST STARTING.
3
My Own Mind Productions presents...
Rhondapunzel
a fantasy sequence by Rhonda Bleenie
YAY! GO ME!
VOICE-OVER: Once upon a time, in a distant land...
... there was an enchanted castle.
And in a tower, high above the castle walls, was a prisoner...
... the beautiful girl known only as Rhondapunzel.

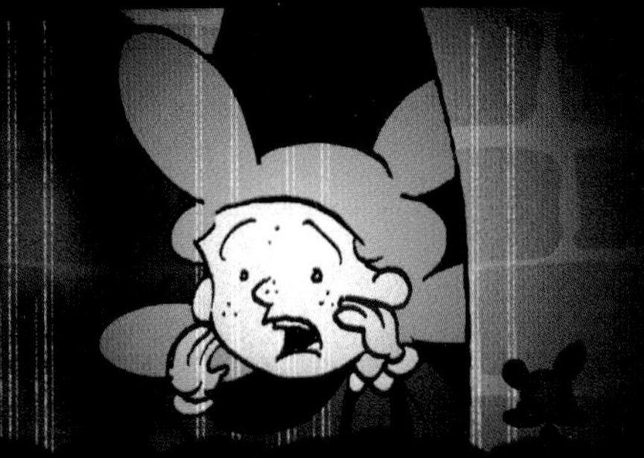

RHONDAPUNZEL: Help! Help! I, Rhondapunzel, am trapped in this tower, and in need of rescuing. (Eligible princes only need apply.)

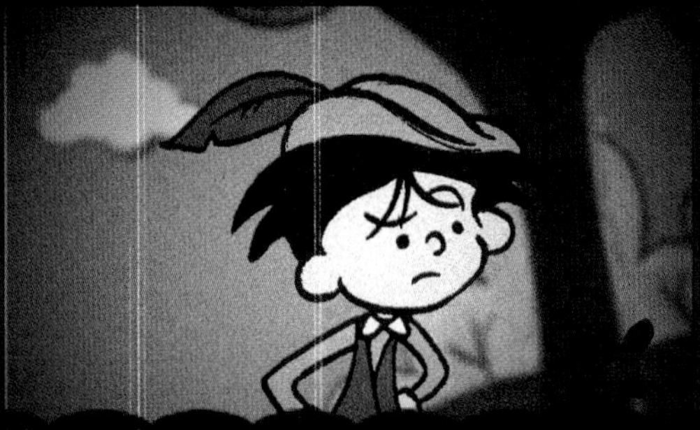

REGINALD: Hark! What doth cometh on yon morn breeze? Zounds! 'Tis the cry of a hot chick in distress!

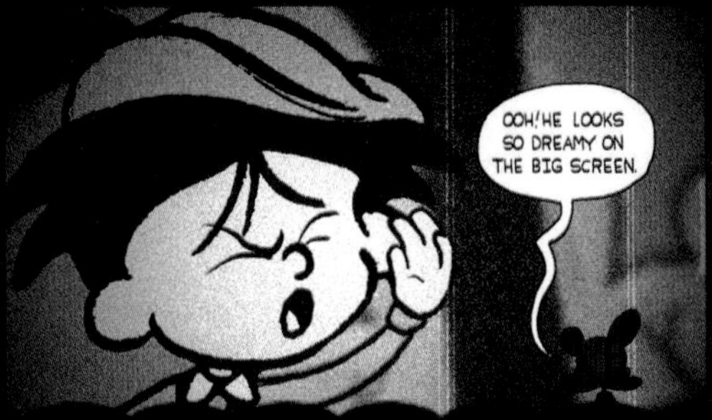
OOH! HE LOOKS SO DREAMY ON THE BIG SCREEN.

REGINALD: Fear not, fair hottie! For Reginald of the Woods is here! Lower your hair and I shall climb up to rescue you anon!

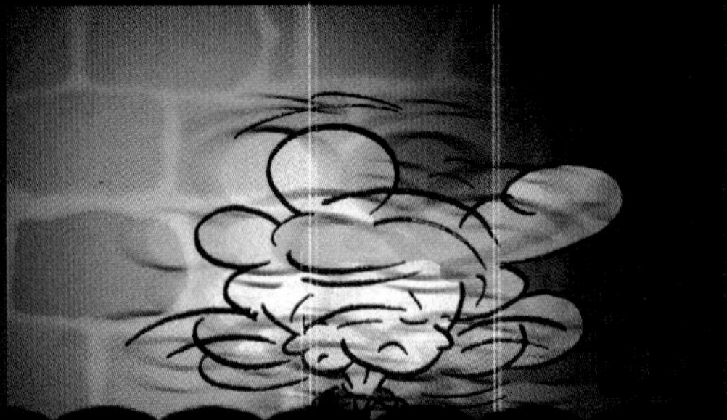

SFX: (Whip Whip Whip)

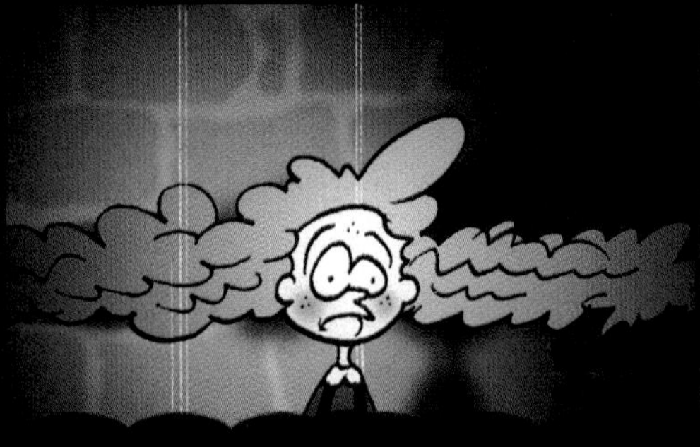

SFX: (Sproing!)
RHONDAPUNZEL: How embarrassing!

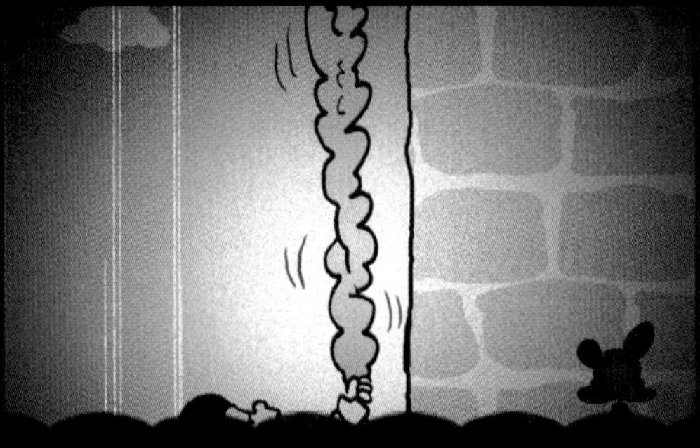

SFX: (Tug Tug)

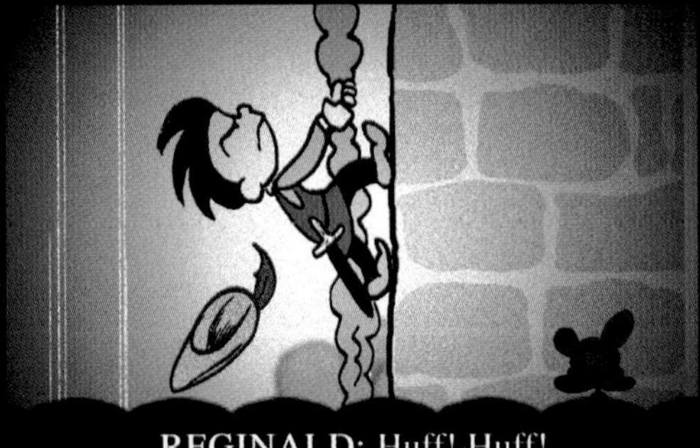

REGINALD: Huff! Huff!

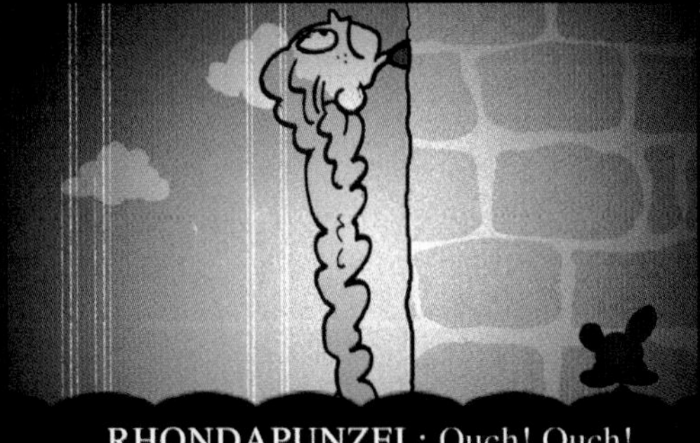

RHONDAPUNZEL: Ouch! Ouch!

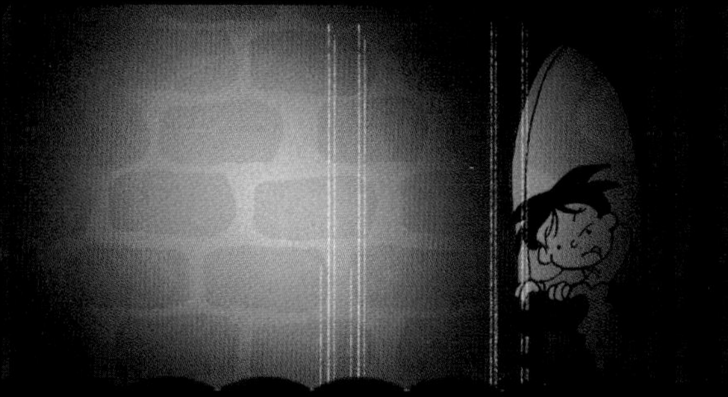

REGINALD: Take heart, fair maiden! For I, Reginald of the Woods, have come to save you.

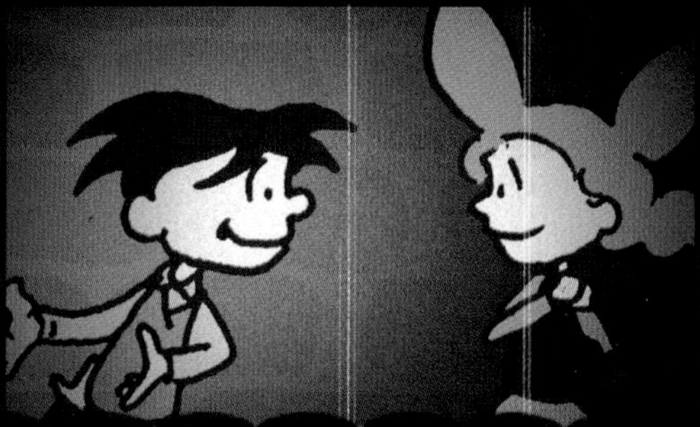

RHONDAPUNZEL: I knew that if I waited long enough, a handsome prince would come to rescue me.

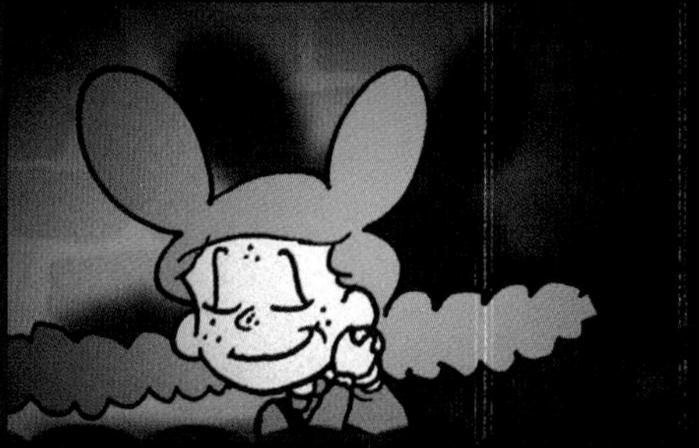

RHONDAPUNZEL: You ARE a prince, aren't you?

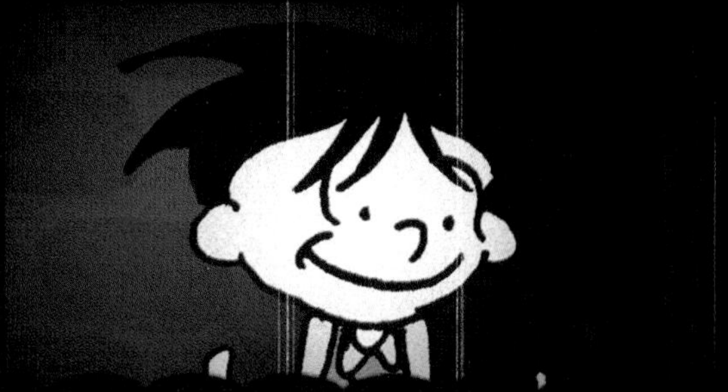

REGINALD: Well, not exactly, but my dad has most of his albums.

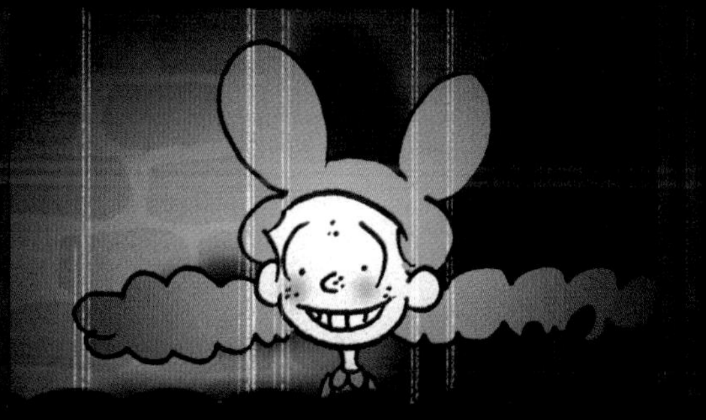

RHONDAPUNZEL: Close enough!

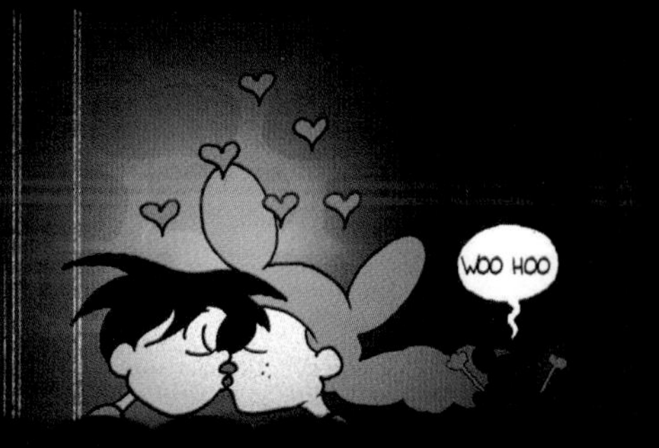
WOO HOO

SFX: Smoooooooooooooch!!

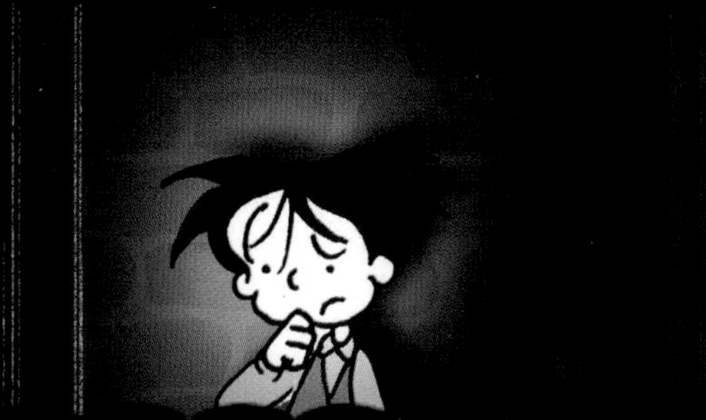

REGINALD: Hmmm...I just thought of something.
RHONDAPUNZEL: Yes, my love?

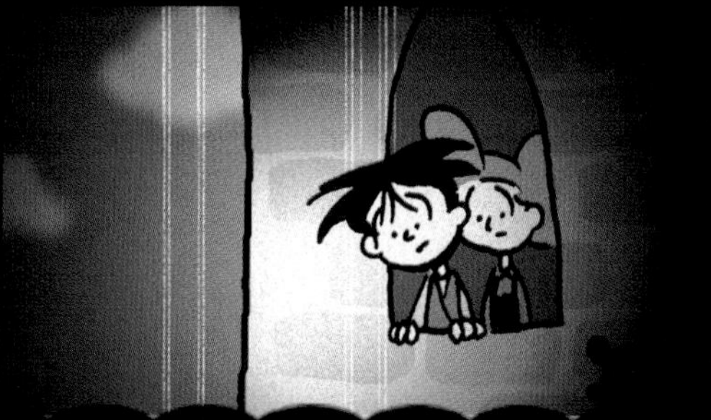

REGINALD: Now that I've rescued you, who is gonna rescue me?

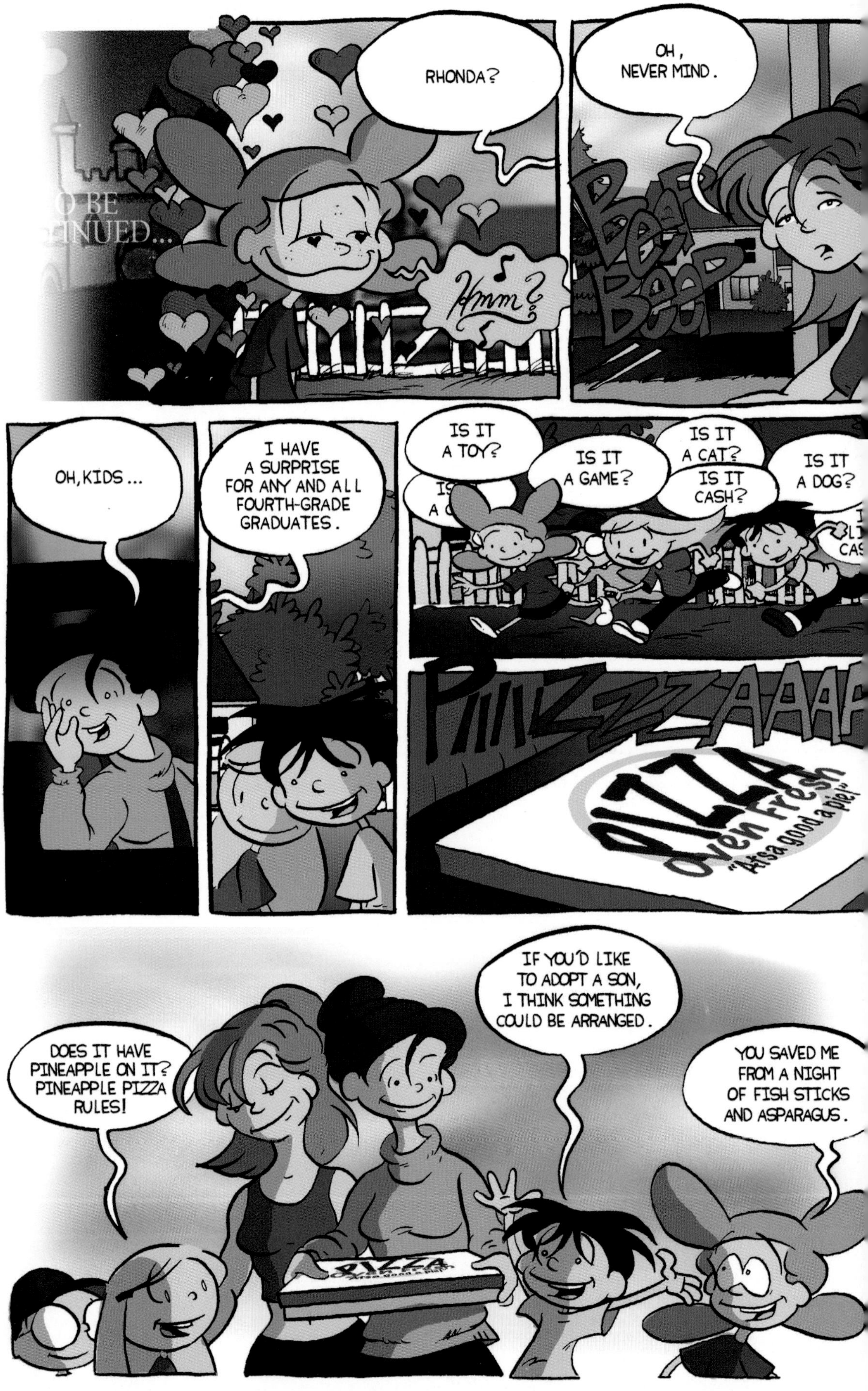
RHONDA?
Hmm?
OH, NEVER MIND.
BEEP BEEP
OH, KIDS ...
I HAVE A SURPRISE FOR ANY AND ALL FOURTH-GRADE GRADUATES.
IS IT A TOY?
IS IT A GAME?
IS IT A CAT?
IS IT CASH?
IS IT A DOG?
PIZZA
oven fresh
"Atsa good a pie!"
DOES IT HAVE PINEAPPLE ON IT? PINEAPPLE PIZZA RULES!
IF YOU'D LIKE TO ADOPT A SON, I THINK SOMETHING COULD BE ARRANGED.
YOU SAVED ME FROM A NIGHT OF FISH STICKS AND ASPARAGUS.

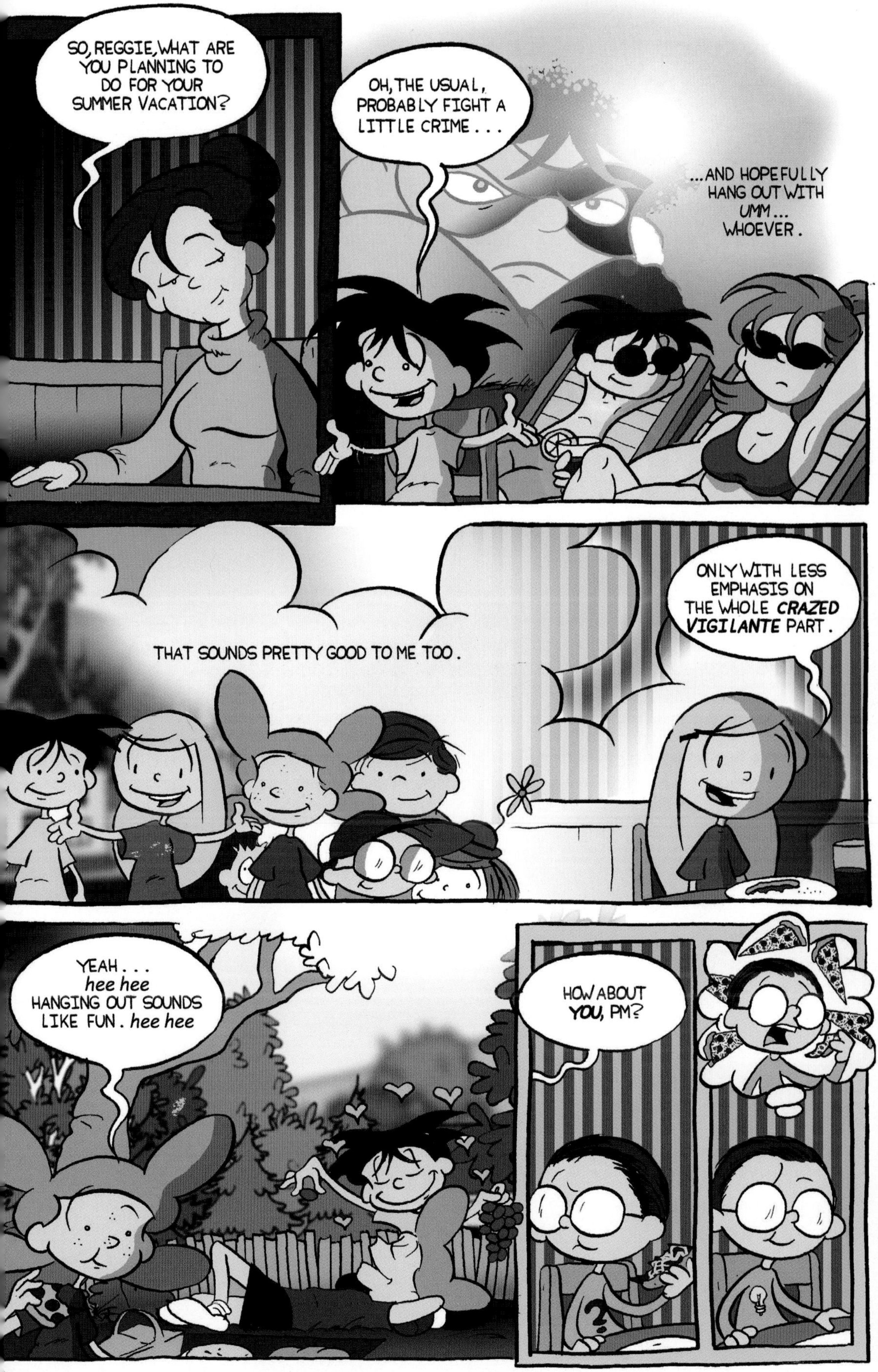
SO, REGGIE, WHAT ARE YOU PLANNING TO DO FOR YOUR SUMMER VACATION?
OH, THE USUAL, PROBABLY FIGHT A LITTLE CRIME . . .
...AND HOPEFULLY HANG OUT WITH UMM... WHOEVER.
THAT SOUNDS PRETTY GOOD TO ME TOO.
ONLY WITH LESS EMPHASIS ON THE WHOLE CRAZED VIGILANTE PART.
YEAH . . . hee hee HANGING OUT SOUNDS LIKE FUN. hee hee
HOW ABOUT YOU, PM?

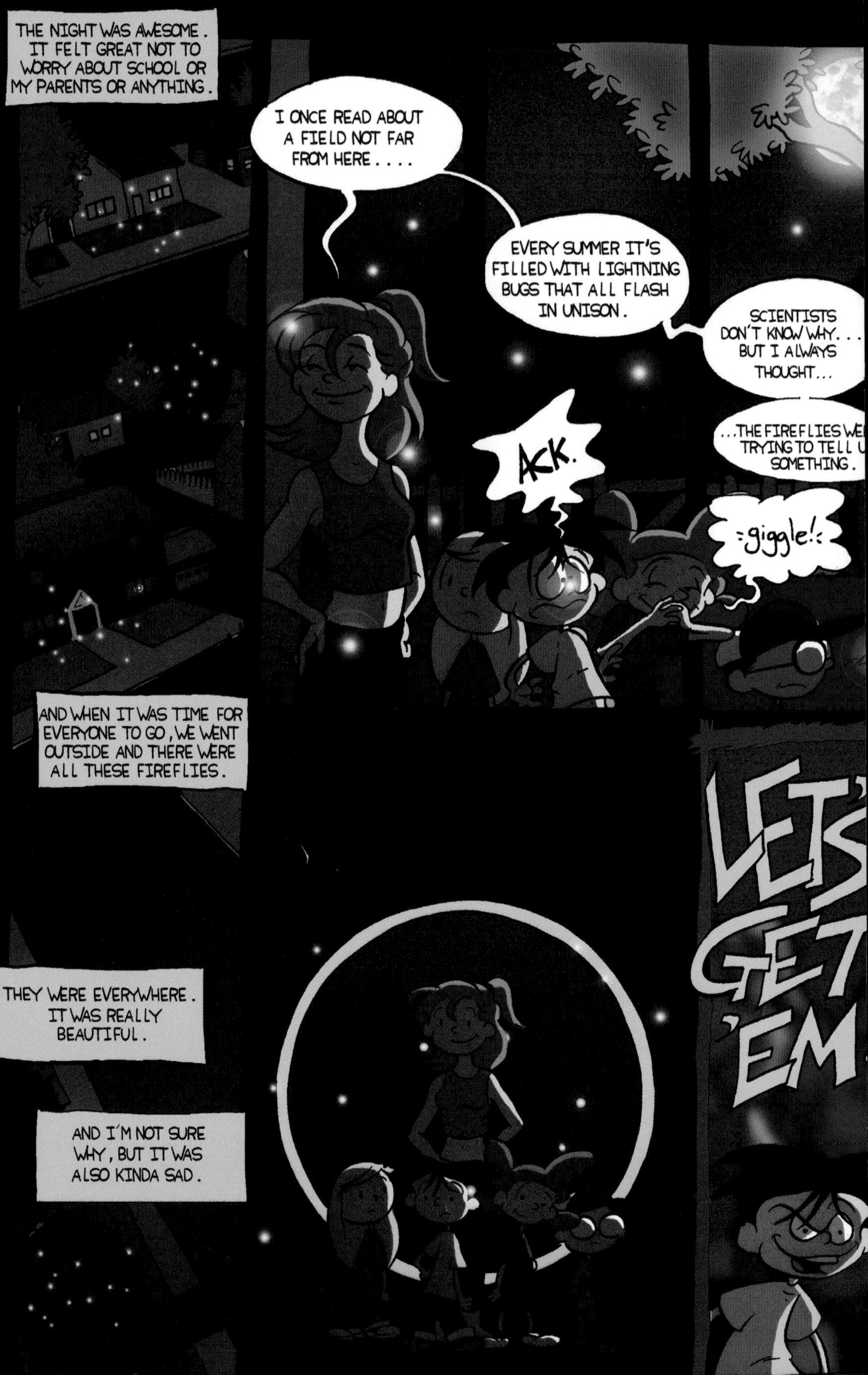
THE NIGHT WAS AWESOME. IT FELT GREAT NOT TO WORRY ABOUT SCHOOL OR MY PARENTS OR ANYTHING.
I ONCE READ ABOUT A FIELD NOT FAR FROM HERE....
EVERY SUMMER IT'S FILLED WITH LIGHTNING BUGS THAT ALL FLASH IN UNISON.
SCIENTISTS DON'T KNOW WHY... BUT I ALWAYS THOUGHT...
ACK.
:giggle!:
AND WHEN IT WAS TIME FOR EVERYONE TO GO, WE WENT OUTSIDE AND THERE WERE ALL THESE FIREFLIES.
THEY WERE EVERYWHERE. IT WAS REALLY BEAUTIFUL.
AND I'M NOT SURE WHY, BUT IT WAS ALSO KINDA SAD.

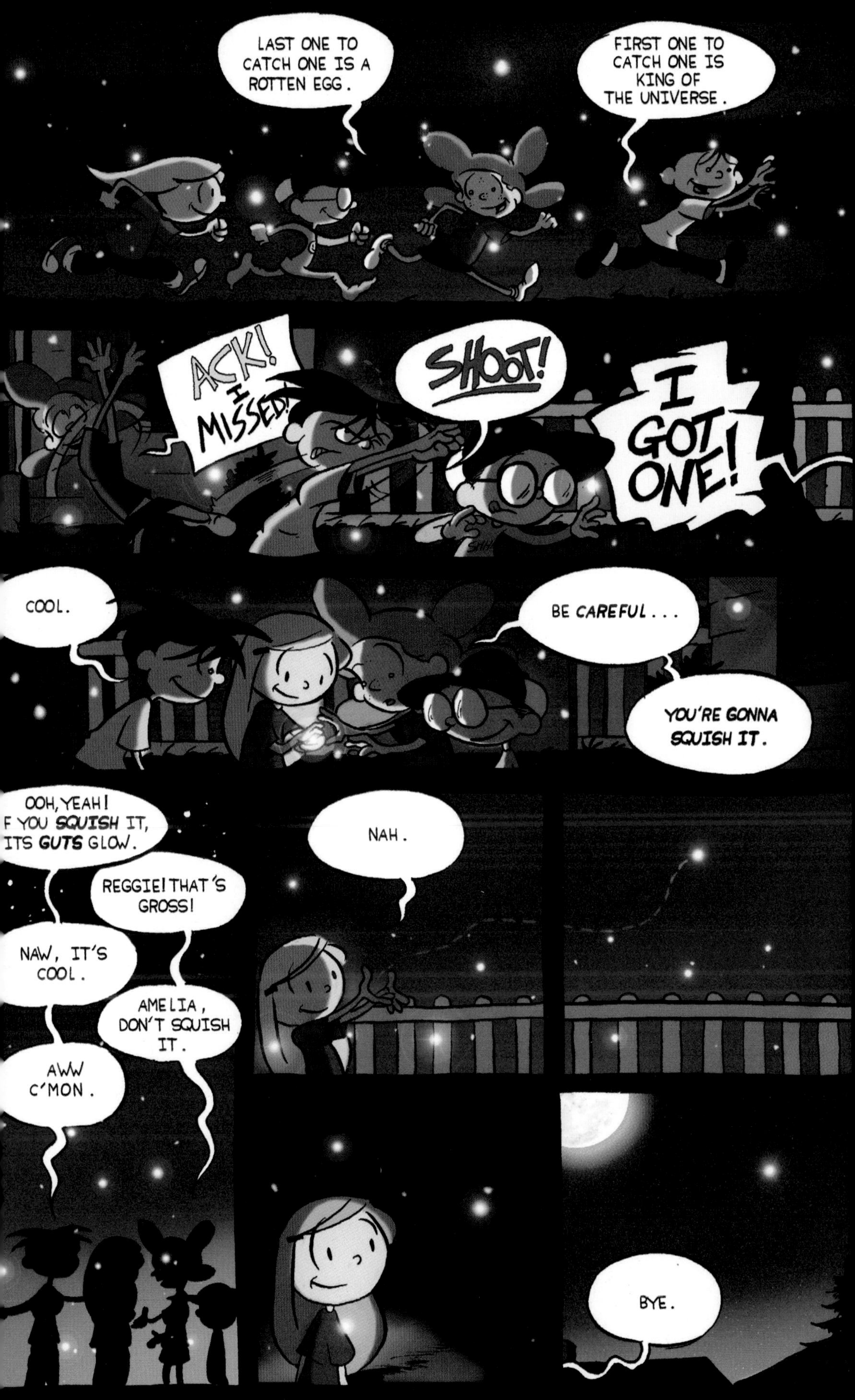
LAST ONE TO CATCH ONE IS A ROTTEN EGG.
FIRST ONE TO CATCH ONE IS KING OF THE UNIVERSE.
ACK! I MISSED!
SHOOT!
I GOT ONE!
COOL.
BE CAREFUL . . .
YOU'RE GONNA SQUISH IT.
OOH, YEAH! F YOU SQUISH IT, ITS GUTS GLOW.
REGGIE! THAT'S GROSS!
NAW, IT'S COOL.
AMELIA, DON'T SQUISH IT.
AWW C'MON.
NAH.
BYE.

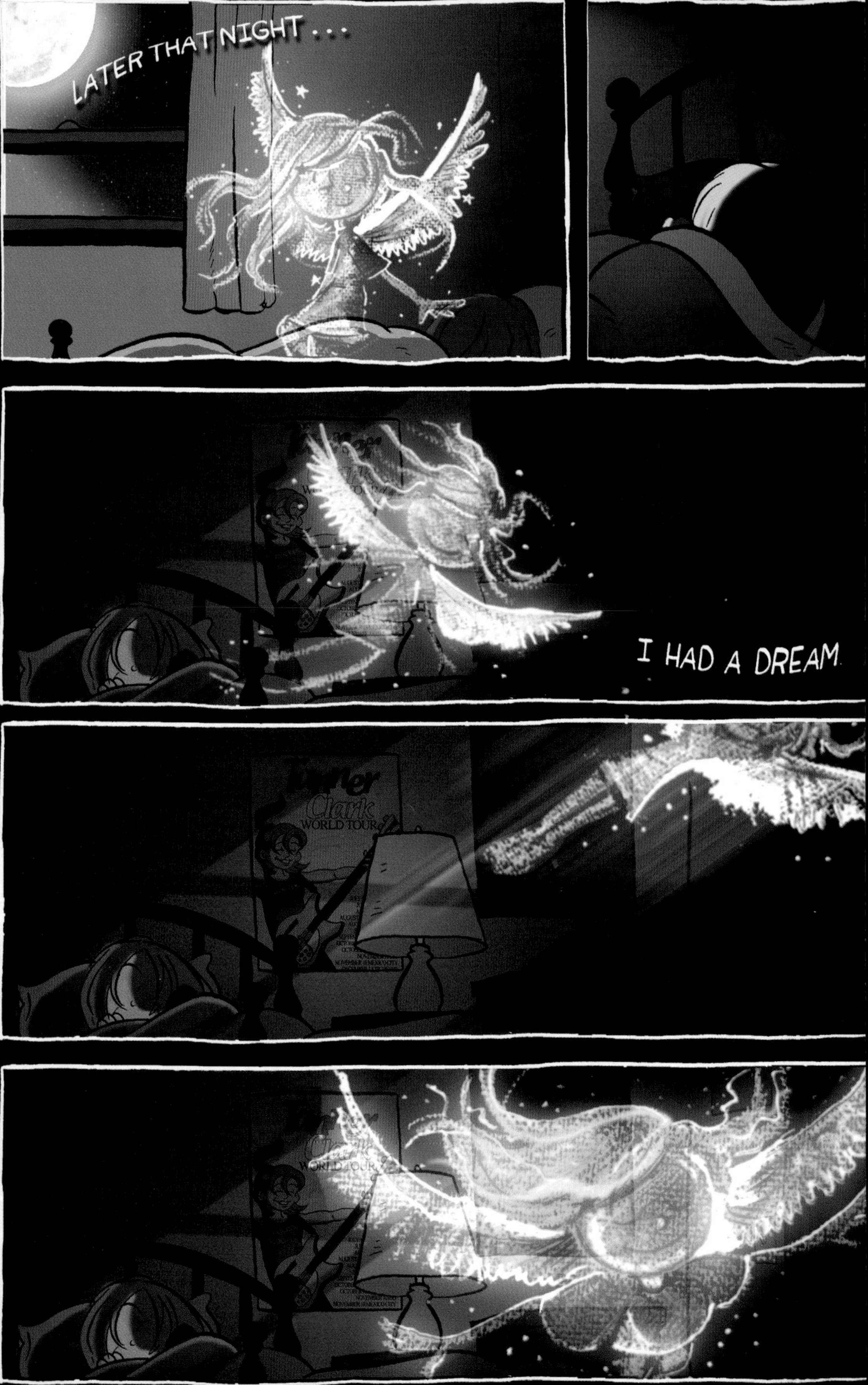
LATER THAT NIGHT . . .
I HAD A DREAM.
Clark
WORLD TOUR

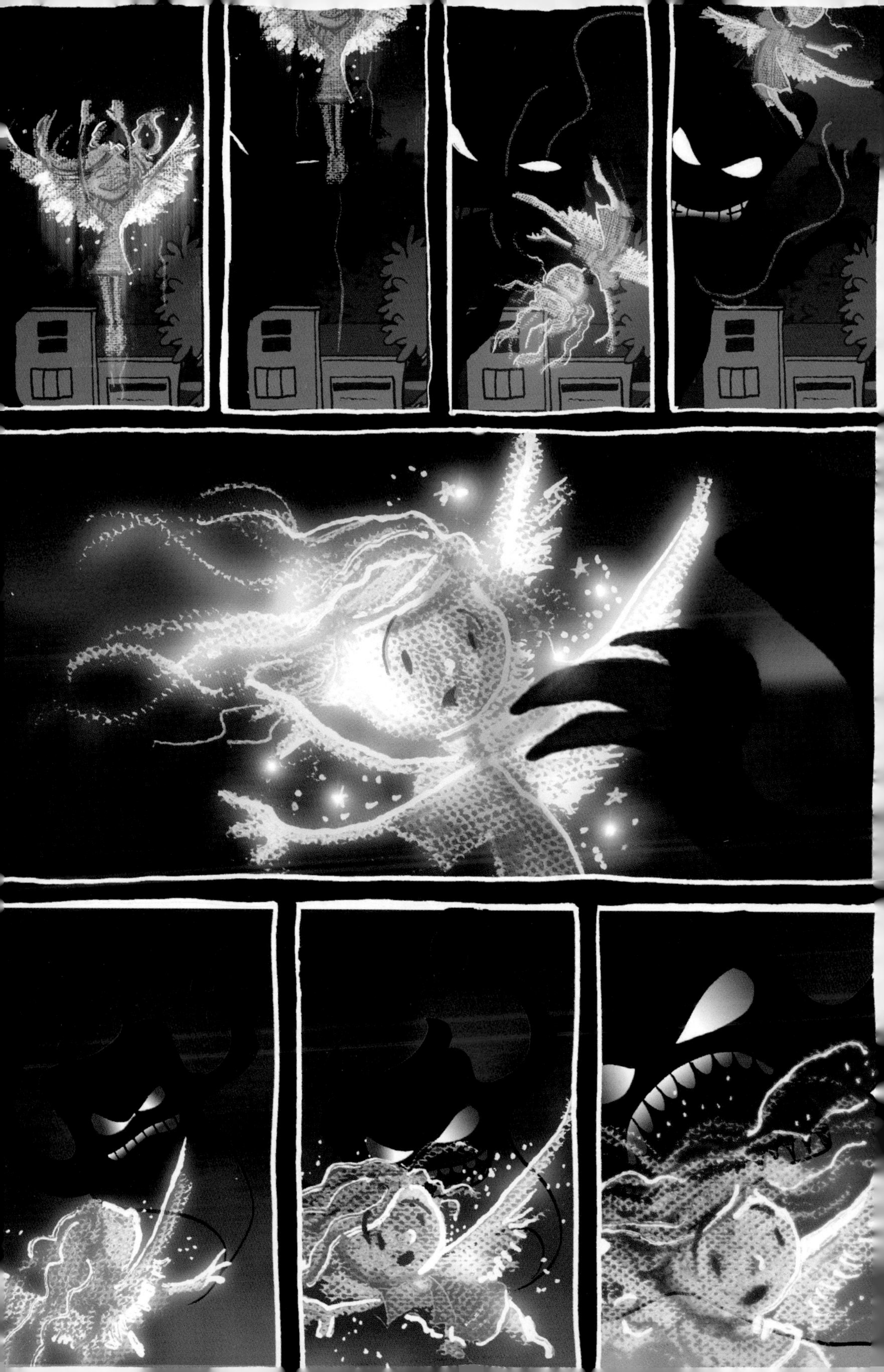

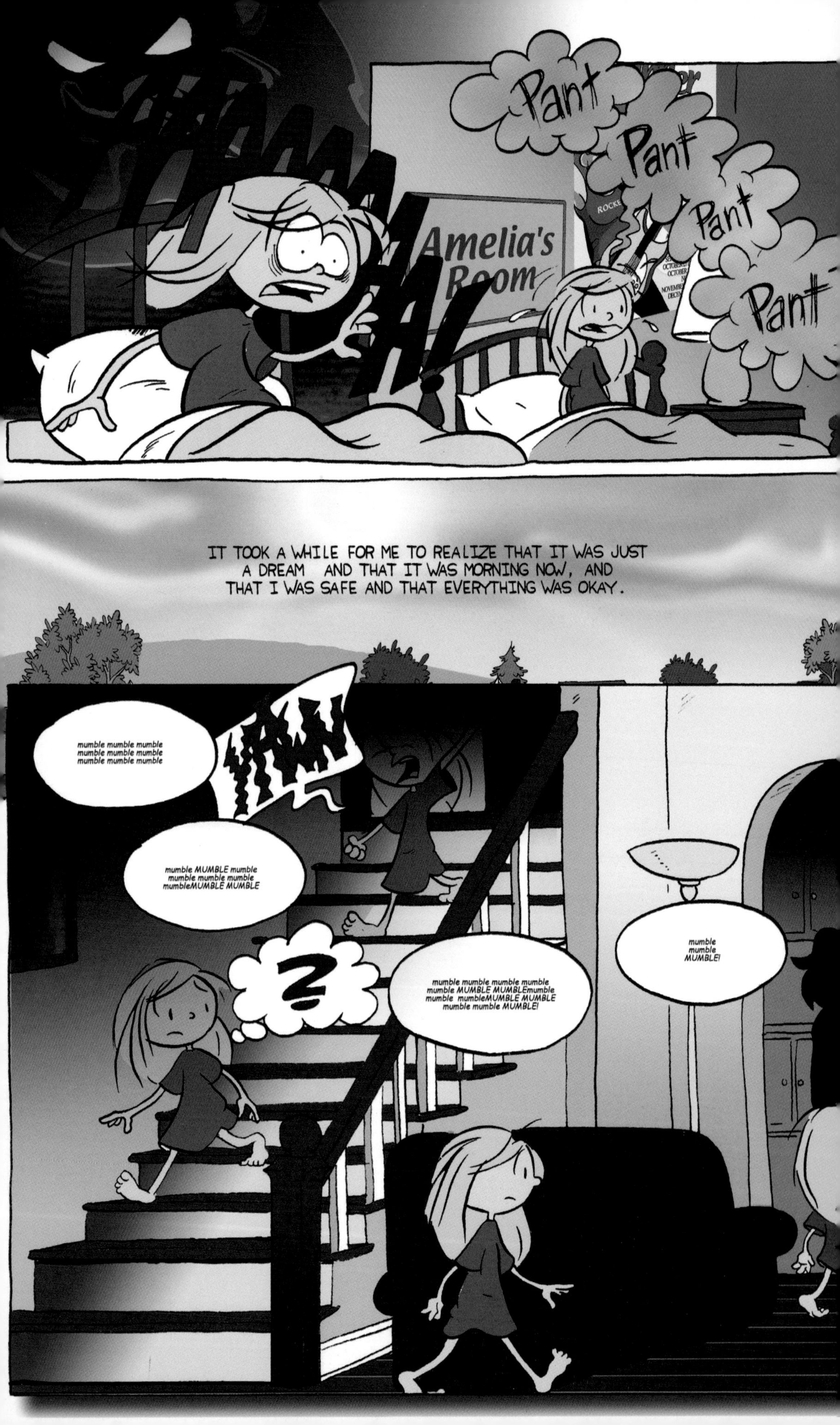
Amelia's Room
Pant
Pant
Pant
Pant
IT TOOK A WHILE FOR ME TO REALIZE THAT IT WAS JUST A DREAM AND THAT IT WAS MORNING NOW, AND THAT I WAS SAFE AND THAT EVERYTHING WAS OKAY.
mumble mumble mumble mumble mumble mumble mumble mumble mumble
YAWN
mumble MUMBLE mumble mumble mumble mumble mumbleMUMBLE MUMBLE
Z
mumble mumble mumble mumble mumble MUMBLE MUMBLEmumble mumble mumbleMUMBLE MUMBLE mumble mumble MUMBLE!
mumble mumble MUMBLE!

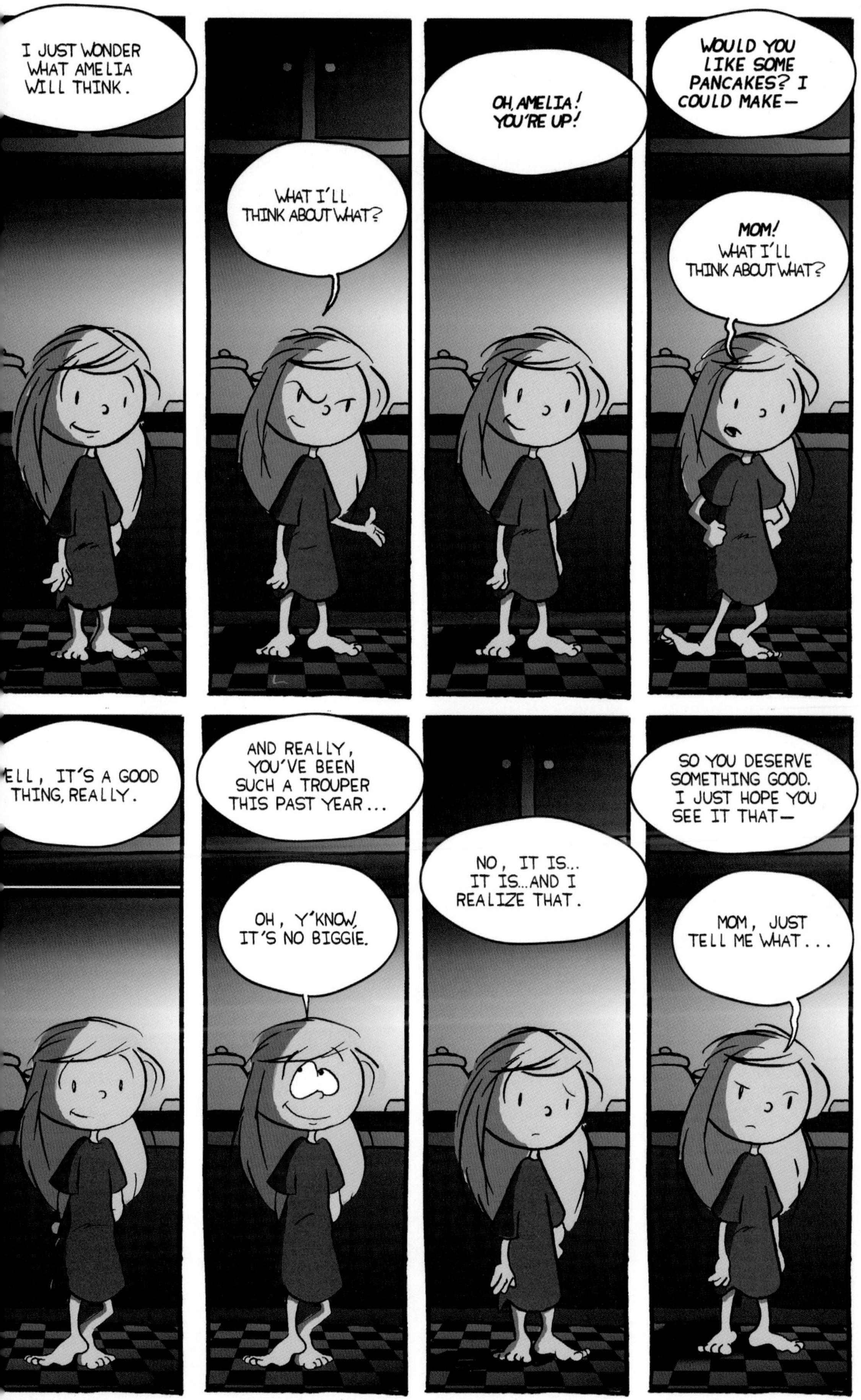
I JUST WONDER WHAT AMELIA WILL THINK.
WHAT I'LL THINK ABOUT WHAT?
OH, AMELIA! YOU'RE UP!
WOULD YOU LIKE SOME PANCAKES? I COULD MAKE—
MOM! WHAT I'LL THINK ABOUT WHAT?
ELL, IT'S A GOOD THING, REALLY.
AND REALLY, YOU'VE BEEN SUCH A TROUPER THIS PAST YEAR...
OH, Y'KNOW, IT'S NO BIGGIE.
NO, IT IS... IT IS...AND I REALIZE THAT.
SO YOU DESERVE SOMETHING GOOD. I JUST HOPE YOU SEE IT THAT—
MOM, JUST TELL ME WHAT...

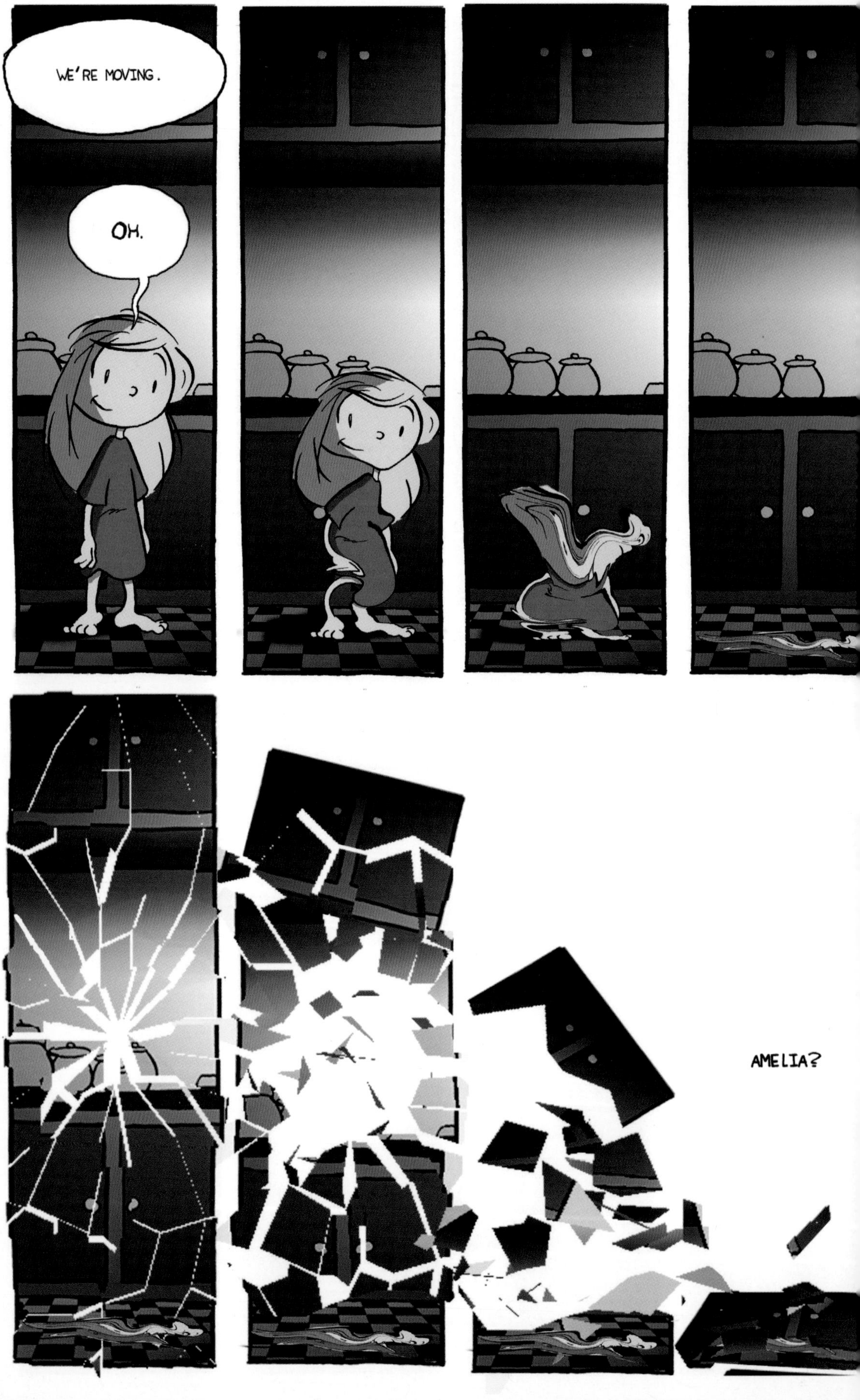
WE'RE MOVING.
OH.
AMELIA?

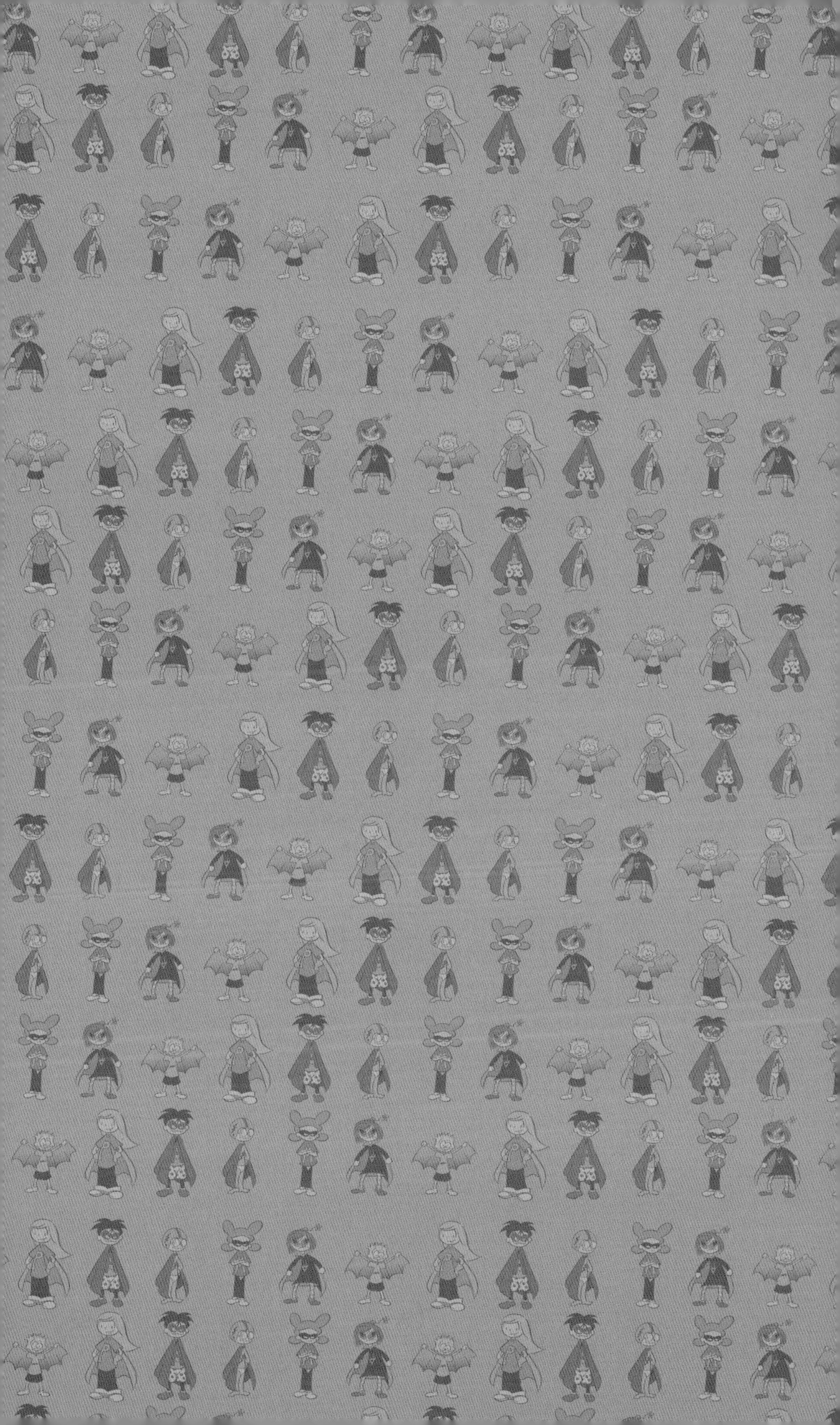